THE IRISH PRINCE

THE BILLIONAIRE DYNASTIES

THE IRISH PRINCE

THE BILLIONAIRE DYNASTIES

VIRGINIA NELSON

Entangled Publishing, LLC
2614 South Timberline Road
Suite 109
Fort Collins, CO 80525
Visit our website at www.entangledpublishing.com.

Indulgence is an imprint of Entangled Publishing, LLC.

Edited by Stephen Morgan
Cover design by Bree Archer
Cover art from iStock

Manufactured in the United States of America

First Edition May 2017

Dedicated to Barb, Stacey, and Lisa. Thanks for all your kind words during the early pages of this! I got to work with you by chance but got lucky because you're all amazing!!

Chapter One

Chelsea

She'd quit for real this time. It seemed she thought about it a hundred times a day lately, so finding a lacy bra hanging over the back of her chair was yet another sign from the universe that she should just do it. But he paid well, dammit, and she was under contract, something he reminded her of every time she tried to tender her resignation, which was something she'd tried to do at least four times in the last month. The man drove her crazy, had been driving her crazy for years. And every time she quit, he somehow managed to take back her resignation and convince her to stay.

But not this time. She was done. With all of it.

No matter how charming or beguiling Aiden Kelley was, Chelsea was serious about quitting this time. She wasn't going to let him convince her otherwise.

"So you're really leaving?" Her friend Kimmie's voice through her headset pulled her out of her thoughts and back to their conversation. "What did he do this time?"

"I'm definitely leaving, and I told him so this morning," she insisted. "I found a bra in my office this morning. And it sure isn't one of mine."

Kimmie's laughter came through clear. "He's crossdressing now?"

Chelsea grabbed her bowl of rocks and sat at the desk, shuffling through the stones to soothe herself. "I wouldn't put it past him, and the bastard has good enough legs that he'd probably pull it off. No, I think he 'entertained' someone in my office last night, or at least he used my office as a pit stop on the way through to his."

A pink piece of quartz captured her attention, so she pulled it out to rub while she talked.

The sound of chewing preceded Kimmie's answer. "So the Irish Prince was getting down and dirty on your desk? Please tell me he left behind an ass print on the mahogany. Send me a pic of that, and I will become instantly social media famous. Pretty please, Chelsea-girl? Do a girl a solid."

She jerked back from the desk in question and peered at it suspiciously. *No…*

"He wouldn't have done her on my desk," Chelsea said aloud, not sure if she was trying to convince herself or Kimmie. "And quit calling him that. He hates that stupid name. It is all Camden James's fault. If he had fought harder against that asinine name the press gave him, they wouldn't be naming all the rich guys after princes. Not to mention, Aiden isn't Irish. At least, I don't think he is."

"The newspapers disagree," Kimmie pointed out. "Is there an ass print? I know you looked."

The door to Chelsea's office opened slowly, and Lucy peered in. Chelsea sat up straighter and put the pink rock back in the bowl. "Can I help you, Lucy?"

"Aawww, she got busted talking about her boss getting laid on her desk," Kimmie chirped in her ear. Chelsea covered the device with her hand, not that Lucy could hear her friend. But just in case.

"There is someone here to see Mr. Kelley..." Lucy began.

"You know as well as I do that he is booked solid for weeks, Lucy. Tell them to give us a call and schedule an appointment." Really, she shouldn't have to tell Lucy that, since Lucy had worked for the firm long enough to know how Mr. Kelley liked things. He didn't do spontaneous pop-in visits and didn't like anything he hadn't planned for in advance. It was all part of his control-freak nature. Chelsea suspected it might go deeper than just him wanting to be in charge of everything—like anxiety disorder or something—but she'd long ago decided looking too closely into Aiden Kelley's personality would only end badly.

"I tried that, Chelsea. She insists." Lucy gnawed her adorable bottom lip, looking like a model off an ad for makeup.

"She?" Ah, so it was one of Aiden's many paramours. Usually, a stern *no* had them returning home, tails tucked between their legs. *Their apparently panty-less legs*, a snide part of her brain snuck in. "Lucy, explain to whomever it is that—"

Someone pushed the door the rest of the way open, and a red-haired woman glared at Chelsea. "He can fit me in."

Chelsea recognized her immediately, but then again, who wouldn't recognize America's Sweetheart? "Uh, Ms. Welles," Chelsea began. "I apologize, but if you'll give me a moment, I'm sure we can find a place in his schedule—"

"Look, maybe he won't make time for me." Margo Welles stepped aside, revealing a young girl. "But if not me, I'm sure he'll make time for her."

The girl had curly hair and sculpted cheekbones that assured she would grow into a great beauty. Aiden must have had the same cheekbones when he was a kid. God knew he was impossibly attractive now—

Wait.

No.

It can't...

She looked again at the girl and saw an uncanny resemblance.

Holy...

Now Chelsea knew why Margo Welles would want to see Aiden. She sucked in a lungful of air as shock ripped through her. It took her a second, but she found her voice and was proud it didn't waver. "Lucy, cancel Mr. Kelley's appointments for the rest of the morning and work to reschedule them as soon as possible."

• • •

AIDEN

Aiden Kelley had almost become used to fighting a sense of boredom and tedium. He used to have to fight tooth and nail to get what he wanted—born a second-generation Irish kid in the Bronx to a dishwasher and a window washer, there wasn't a lot handed to him on any kind of platter, not to mention silver. But he'd joined the Air Force to get out before coming home and enrolling in business college. He never got around to finishing college. Instead, he'd gotten a job as a sales assistant at Marcy's and used the skills he learned in the military and college to become the best at what he did.

But inventing things? That was an act he felt passionate about. He'd invented a kilt with cargo pockets and shown it to his boss, who'd nixed the idea, calling it unlikely to sell. Motivation wasn't ever one of Aiden's problems, so he simply quit his job and used some money he'd put back as well as a loan from his dad to start his own small business. He sold his kilts to small shops around New York until he landed his first big contract with Marcy's direct competitor.

Basically, he knew how to go from nothing to hit it big, and he'd managed to keep his company going for years now with no problems. Which, ironically, turned out to be the problem. He was bored silly. Nothing was really at risk any more.

Until Margo showed up claiming that Waverley was his daughter and she wanted money. Not a lot of money—which shocked Aiden more than the claim of a child, really. Just enough to ensure they could continue to live comfortably. The modeling jobs were spaced out, dwindling as Margo aged, because being a model had an expiration date. She wanted security for Waverley's future until she figured out her next steps in life, which wasn't even a bad thing…

It was fair, if the child was his. More than fair, really.

He'd come into the office today, begging the universe to send him a challenge. Something new for him to master. How was he supposed to know it would come in the form of the little girl sitting in his executive assistant's office?

And now that he'd spent a couple of uncomfortable hours in his office, sitting across from Margo, the rush paternity test his wealth had purchased offered all of the proof they needed.

"So Waverley is my daughter," he said.

Margo crossed her arms. "Yeah. And now that you believe me, I need you to give me what I asked for."

Definitely not boring, which should've been a nice change of pace. Instead, she'd flipped him on his ass with her claim. Margo was one of a string of models and actresses in his past, and she'd not stuck out as something that would change his life. As the mother of his child, she should've been exceptionally memorable.

But she wasn't. If he remembered right, they'd hooked up hot and heavy for a short period of time and then ended on reasonably good terms. She'd called him a control freak; he'd shrugged, since the novelty of the chase had worn off the relationship anyway. He hadn't thought about her again in the ten years since their parting.

He was thinking about her now. What would've driven her to raise their child alone? What really sent her to his door at this point? How awful of a person was he that he'd had a daughter out there, growing up without a dad all these years, and didn't know it?

He wasn't sure what he'd seen in her, so many years ago. Most of her movements and mannerisms were so practiced as to seem false. Unlike his assistant, who would lose horribly if she'd taken up gambling rather than business. Chelsea had no ability to filter her expressions, so even when she said the thing she thought he wanted to hear, he could easily read her open face and recognize the truth.

He liked that about Chelsea, actually. Preferred it to model perfection. Margo sat across from him without invitation, which was good as he still hadn't figured out what to say to her.

"You came here asking for money," he said. "You'll excuse me if I want to also discuss the implications of finding out I have a daughter."

"I agreed to the paternity test. The number I gave you was more than fair, so I hope that we can conclude our business rather quickly, Aiden." No tells gave away what Margo was feeling, only that she was cool, calm, and collected.

While Aiden? Felt like there was a war being waged in his brain. His emotions were raw, his thoughts were in chaos, and he had no idea what he wanted to come of this meeting. So he decided to be honest.

"Margo, you've had ten years with our child." He held up a hand when she opened her mouth to speak. "Ten years that I never even knew Waverley existed. I didn't get to name her; I didn't get to buy her gifts; I didn't get to be there for her. I know, you come from money and likely don't comprehend why any of this would matter to me. But it does. She's mine, and you basically stole my ability to be there for her for a decade."

Margo frowned. Clearly, he wasn't reacting in the way that she'd hoped. "And, as I said when you brought me into your office, with a check I can make your life just as it was this morning again. Be realistic here, Aiden. You don't want a child right now. You have a life, a business to run. I'm simply asking for you to make a donation toward her support. This isn't complicated at all."

But it *was* complicated. The child was part of his life but completely unexpected. Part of how he functioned was by controlling situations, knowing what happened next. Doctors called it anxiety disorder, but he just considered it part of who he was. So he liked organization—not a bad thing, generally. He liked routine, schedule, planning…and this situation left his hands shaking and dizziness threatening. Showing any of that to Margo, though, was out of the question.

But easy as the answer seemed—just let Margo keep handling the situation—it wasn't acceptable to him. Aiden's dad was one of the most important people in his life. He'd been there when Aiden wanted to enlist and cried when he'd sworn into the service. He'd loaned Aiden part of the money to start his business. His dad was amazing, hands down the best father Aiden could've hoped for.

And Aiden would die before he failed to live up to that example. Hell, Margo had stolen away his parents' only grandchild, too. All in all, her crimes against him were heinous.

All that said, attacking the model wasn't going to fix any of it. This woman had raised his child, albeit without his consent, and Waverley likely loved her mother. Fighting with her would only distance him further from the child who thought of him as a stranger.

That was it! He needed time with Waverley. "What if I

agree to your request, but I have some terms of my own?"

Margo raised an eyebrow. "Such as?"

"You've had ten years with her, and I want some time. I want a chance to get to know her. I'll give you every dime you asked for and then some, but I want to be a part of her life going forward."

Margo sat back in her chair, looking surprised. "You want to be part of her life?"

He nodded. Now that he'd thought of it, it was the only thing that would do. The only way he could hope to make something good out of what was a very shitty situation. It wasn't much control, but it was a handhold. A way up the cliff out of disorder back into rational ordered life…via a scheduled visitation or something to that effect. Just the thought calmed his racing pulse, eased the churning in his stomach.

"If I agree, you'll give me the money?" Margo added.

"Every dime and then some," he repeated.

Sliding one leg over the other to cross them elegantly, Margo seemed to consider his request. Realistically, she had to recognize that any refusal on her part would simply begin a war. Now that he knew he had a child, he wasn't letting her walk back out of his life. He'd take Margo to court if he had to and to hell with the press and consequences. He'd rather, though, settle the situation amicably.

Hopefully, Margo would come to the same conclusion.

"I have a demand of my own, then," Margo finally said.

"You already demanded money and stole my child for ten years. What more can you ask for?" The words weren't intended to come out quite so venomous, but he spoke with his emotions rather than his logic. He raised a hand again, asking her silently to give him a second, before adding, "That was harsh, and I'm sorry. My emotions got the best of me. What more would you like me to do, Margo?"

Her frown didn't vanish, but she sighed. "Waverley is a bit

of a rock hound. Loves all things geology, and with work… I've never managed to take her to the Grand Canyon. You want to get to know her; she wants to see the Canyon. Take her to see it, and we'll arrange further visitation from there."

He held out his hand. "Deal."

Only as Margo shook and confirmed the arrangement did he realize what he'd agreed to.

Now to figure out how to go from the world's most eligible bachelor to the world's greatest dad in a single weekend.

Chapter Two

Chelsea

The little girl sitting in Chelsea's office looked bored to tears. Then again, she was only about ten, so sitting in the black leather chair probably would bore a kid. Especially when she'd been waiting for two hours. What were Aiden and Margo talking about, anyway? And leaving the girl with Chelsea? She was a secretary, not a babysitter.

His daughter had the look of her father, though, especially right around the eyes—both in their shape and the hazel color, although her heavy, dark eyebrows weren't as well-groomed as his. Her hair, though...that had to be from her model-slash-actress mother. The vivid red waves were the trademark of the adult woman—her halo of flame-colored curls graced a lot of magazine covers, after all, over the years—but on the child, it'd been tamed into two tight French braids.

The fact the kid was so disinterested and unoccupied and yet managed to only swing her skinny little legs at an even pace while keeping her fingers neatly folded in her lap—well, the self-possession and control were like a neon sign proclaiming the child a Kelley. She'd never met a bigger control freak than Aiden, so it would only make sense that he'd pass down that annoying trait when he spawned.

Chelsea could see it, making it likely that the girl was indeed the daughter of her boss, philanthropist and executive in charge of a global enterprise, the famed Aiden Kelley. That his ex, Margo Wells, famous in her own right, had managed to keep the kid a secret for a decade was the part that dinged alarm bells, in Chelsea's opinion. Why would she hide their child from Aiden? More importantly, *how* had she kept the child hidden from the press?

But it wasn't Chelsea's place to verbalize these questions. After all, she was the executive assistant to Kelley, not an interviewer. Knowing she didn't have the right and tamping down on her natural curiosity were two very different things, though, and she snuck peeks at the kid every few seconds.

The child was quiet, simply rocking her legs and waiting quite patiently for someone so young—then again, maybe that was normal for a ten-year-old. It wasn't like Chelsea had spent much time around children. She spent most of her waking hours working or thinking about working, which left little time for socializing, and even if she had spare time…she didn't really like kids for the most part. Too noisy. Too messy. Too something people had if they were in a relationship, which she distinctly was not.

And damn, wasn't she broody today? Sipping her coffee, she cast another glance at the kid and noticed she was poking at the dish of rocks on the table near the chair. Ah, her Zen rock garden. She'd collected the stones on a whim. Chelsea used to like that sort of thing when she was younger, and the pretty colors made her smile—but the kid seemed really interested. She carefully picked them up, one after the other, inspecting them with rapt attention.

"Amethyst," Chelsea finally said, gesturing to the purple rock in the kid's hand. It wasn't like Aiden told her not to talk to her when he arbitrarily dropped her off in Chelsea's office, after all.

The child looked up—what had they said her name was? Waverley? Was that even a name?

"Yes," the kid said. "This is a really nice piece of amethyst. There is a cartoon with a character named Amethyst, and she's a crystal gem. Are these your rocks?"

Ah, well, that was a regular conversation starter. Couldn't hurt to chat a bit. She stood and headed over. "Yes, they are, and thanks for the compliment. Did you see the quartz point?" She pointed at a creamy translucent rock, shaped like a crystal.

"I sure did!" Waverley picked up the rock in question and considered it closely. "This is a big one."

"Do you like rocks?" Chelsea asked, sitting down at the chair opposite Waverley.

"I do. I'm going to be a geologist someday. I'm going to travel the world and see all the best rocks." The child's chin came up in an expression so like her father's that it could've passed for a paternity test.

"That's cool. I used to want to be one myself. What other rocks do you recognize?" The child picked through the bowl, lifting up various rocks and identifying them on sight. She knew jade, rose quartz, and pyrite right off.

She pulled out an orange rock and scrunched her brow. "I don't recognize this one."

"May I?" Chelsea held out her palm, and Waverley passed her the rock. "This is carnelian. It is a member of the quartz family. One of my favorites, actually. I like orange."

"Me too," Waverley said with a grin. She was reaching for another rock when the door connecting Chelsea's office to Aiden's opened, and her parents came out. Her smile faded fast, squashed by the sight of the dark expressions on her parents' faces.

Chelsea couldn't hold her smile, either. His brief smile when he saw them faded, revealing a man shaken to the core. She knew he got anxious in situations where he wasn't in control, and learning about a daughter he hadn't known about for a decade would be enough to throw even a non-control freak into a panic, she guessed. For the sake of Waverley, though, she stretched her lips into what she hoped was a warm grin. "It was nice meeting you, Waverley."

The little girl nodded and ran to her mother's side.

"We'll be right back," Margo said. "I just need a moment to speak with my daughter."

Chelsea didn't miss the choice of words. Not *our child.* Well, Margo couldn't be too fond of Aiden if she'd kept their kid a secret for so long.

Once they'd vanished out the door, Aiden dragged a hand through his dark curls.

The man was handsome, even when he was disturbed. It just wasn't fair that he was that damn hot and that impossibly out of reach all at the same time.

Men like Aiden Kelley didn't notice women like Chelsea Houston. Or, rather, they did notice them—for their usefulness in the business world, for their brains, for their ability to problem solve and deal with tricky situations. They didn't notice them as women, which was kind of a bummer, since she couldn't help noticing him as a man.

A very fine man, who would be a hell of a lot of fun out of his business suit.

Not that she would ever find out. In two weeks, she'd never see him again.

Speaking of…

"Mr. Kelley, I know this isn't a great time, but I need to remind you—"

"We have to reformat my entire schedule." He turned around and walked back into his office.

Okay, guess he expects me to follow him.

"Mr. Kelley, stop, I need to tell you—"

"Cancel all my meetings this week." He sat at his desk and turned to his computer screen. "Any lunches. Any dinners. I can't make them. I'm taking Waverley to the Grand Canyon. And I'll need you to come along with me."

She stopped cold. She knew nothing about kids, and traveling with her boss and his sudden child ranked really low on her to do list. She'd rather pluck out her own toenails.

Once she'd picked her jaw up from the floor, she said, "No. I can't go with you."

He tapped away on his keyboard. "Of course you can. I realize it's outside the office, but it's no different than any of the other duties you've accomplished during your tenure—"

"Aiden. I can't."

Her using his first name? That got his attention.

He turned away from his computer screen and looked at her. "Okay, Chelsea. Why can't you?"

"Because, as already I told you today, I quit."

Chapter Three

Chelsea

It took a real sucker for punishment to want to stay in the room and watch the awkward conversation between Aiden and his newfound daughter, but Chelsea was exactly that variety of fool. At least, she was until she became the topic of conversation.

Waverley stuck out her bottom lip, looking sulky, and her father said, "Your mother tells me you're a rock hound. Would you explain that one to me?"

The kid rolled her eyes, shooting a glance at Chelsea as if to non-verbally ask, *Are you seeing what I have to put up with here?* Out loud, however, she just said, "It means I like to collect and categorize various rocks and non-precious gems."

"Huh," said Aiden, looking completely at a loss for a follow-up question. "So, uh, I saw you checking out Chelsea's rock bowl. How would you feel about getting an up close look at some of those rocks by going to the Grand Canyon?"

Waverley shook her head vehemently and looked at her

mom. "I don't want to go on a trip with him, not even to the Canyon. I don't know him, Mom! Why would I want to know him when he's been too busy to come see me before this? Seriously, this is lame."

He probably deserved that from her perspective, even if he hadn't chosen to abandon her for most of her life. Thankfully, he bit back on his frustrations with Margo and instead focused on his daughter. "I'd really like to get to know you, though, Waverley."

The child looked stubborn, and Chelsea didn't blame her. "I'm not going to change my mind." She looked away from both of her parents, as stubborn as her father. When she saw Chelsea, her face lit up, and Chelsea saw that same conniving smile that so often signaled Aiden knew what he wanted and wouldn't be denied. "Hey, if I actually have to go to the Grand Canyon with you, does that mean Chelsea can come? I'll go if she goes."

She turned to Aiden, already angry at him, like he'd set her up, but to his credit, he was shaking his head. "That's up to Chelsea."

Wow. So the guy could think about someone other than himself. Maybe. If this wasn't some genius strategy to get her to come along anyway.

"I just don't see that being a good idea," Chelsea said. "But tell you what? I'll think about it. If you'll excuse me, I need to go powder my nose."

"What does that mean?" Waverley asked.

Not interested in how Aiden might reply, Chelsea made her exit swiftly. *Shit.* Well, by the time she returned, maybe the father-daughter duo would've abandoned her office, and she could get back to finishing out her two weeks in peace. Scrolling through her phone as she headed to the restrooms, she checked her email really quickly and then noticed a text message from her father.

Her dad? Was awesome. Chelsea was not a lot older than Waverley when her mom passed away and Chelsea's dad took over as a single parent. And, well, he'd rocked at the job, even while Chelsea's mom was still alive but sick. He'd been the kind of father who learned how to braid her hair so that she'd look as "pretty" as her friends. He'd let her polish his nails. Hell, he'd gone shopping with her on more than one occasion. Her dad rocked.

Comparing him to what kind of a father Aiden would become… Shit, the guy was in trouble. There was no way he'd ever manage to go from a perfect stranger to being the kind of father Waverley deserved—that any little girl deserved—without a lot of guidance and support.

But who would help him until he found his way and place in her life?

Not me, she decided. *No way in hell am I signing up for that job.*

There were about a hundred reasons she should back away quickly from the whole situation. For one, Aiden was her boss, but she'd told him she was quitting. And even if she wasn't on her way out the door, mixing business with pleasure was always a bad idea. In this case, her time remaining with the company would be far better spent interviewing possible candidates for her job and then training the new hire. Not gallivanting off on a personal trip with her soon-to-be-former boss.

For two, she was already attracted to the man. She knew that and recognized the weakness it represented. Spending alone time with him, intimate time when the line between boss and employee blurred…unwise, to say the least. It would be one giant mind game with herself to continue to recognize that Aiden was not the man for her.

Even if he did have one of the best asses she'd ever seen in a suit. She couldn't begin to imagine what those broad shoulders of his would look like out of said suit.

Well, hell, that was a lie. She could imagine and had spent many a bored hour between meetings doing just that.

Further, if she agreed to this trip, who would keep things going in the office? Just the day-to-day stuff in the interim would be enough reason for her not to leave the office, especially if he was out and off the map for the duration of his little adventure.

That last one seemed rather feeble, even to herself. But the one reason she couldn't deny? Even if she removed every single reason why dating him was a bad idea, she was gone in two weeks. And as much as she'd love to taste his body as many times as she could before she left, she wasn't about to rock a ship that had just taken on board his newfound daughter.

So, as she rested her hand on her office door, she braced herself to go inside. The answer was a no, plain and simple, nothing more to think about. She simply couldn't afford to cave and agree to go on this trip with Aiden and Waverley.

She opened the door and saw Waverley looking at her father like he was nuts and him pouring the kid a cappuccino. The scone in front of Waverley sat untouched, and the child gazed at Chelsea as if she was a savior—come to rescue her from the inept handling of her well-meaning father.

"Whatcha doing, Aiden?" Chelsea asked, although it looked pretty clear. He was trying to offer his ten-year-old daughter coffee and a scone for lunch.

Although that same lunch would've been top ten on Chelsea's list of lunch favorites, she somehow doubted—both from the kid's expression and logic—that it was typically served to her at home or elsewhere.

"We're about to have lunch. I was hoping you'd join us so we could revisit the Grand Canyon discussion." He looked so damned adorable and unaware as he was fumbling that a piece of her heart melted, just a little.

I know I'm going to regret this.

"I've decided I'll go on the trip." Picking up her office phone, she glanced at Waverley. "What kind of pizza do you like, kid?"

Waverley smiled at her, placing the coffee cup carefully on Chelsea's desk and only sloshing a little onto the shining, ass print-free mahogany. "Pepperoni."

• • •

AIDEN

Once Margo picked up Waverley, promising to bring her back on Friday with her bags packed for the trip and to call him for details in the meantime, Aiden tried to turn the day back to business as usual.

Then again, with Chelsea glaring at him, it was really hard to pretend nothing unusual had happened. He sat behind his desk, she was seated on the other side, and he carefully kept the laptop open between them to block her view of his face.

Not that it worked, but he was trying.

"Okay, regarding the Landon project…did we get the numbers back on that from Greg, or are we still waiting?" He was pleased at his tone—normal, businesslike, completely modulated. He could handle this. He handled everything else.

And to think, his biggest problem only days ago was that he was bored with how easy life had become. He'd trade his left nut to go back to bored, compared to the chaos in his mind at this point.

"Greg got us the numbers, and I have them in front of me. In one click, I can email them to you, and we can both go over them. But if you think for one second we're not going to talk about me quitting before we get to work, you have got another thing coming, buddy." Chelsea's normally calm features weren't calm at all.

If anything, she looked passionate. Filled with fire. Hell, if he were honest, she looked kind of hot, all pissed off like that.

Then again, his assistant never really lost her cool normally. She might get frustrated with him, but regardless of his shenanigans, she maintained a mostly calm demeanor. She'd never worn anything except for the same kind of suit, just in different colors, in all the years he'd known her. Did she own a pair of jeans? Did she have a pair of fuzzy slippers? What was the woman like when she wasn't at work?

Why was he wondering about all of that now? Oh, yeah, because she said she was quitting. All the mysteries about her that he'd never really wondered about before might never be solved. To top matters off, he'd convinced her to go on a trip with him and his daughter that crossed the country. Well, he'd find out about the jeans, he was pretty sure.

"Are you ignoring me?" she asked.

"No, I'm pulling up the numbers from the ad campaign, because we do have a lot of work to get done today. All personal things need to be set aside, especially if we're going to be out of the office for more than a week." He tapped on his keyboard, but he wasn't writing anything. He was just hitting the home row keys repeatedly, hoping to fool her.

"More than a week?" she squeaked. "I figured we would fly out there, maybe stay the weekend, and be back here for work on Monday. Yeah, we really need to talk about this so I can know what you have planned before you tote me across the country."

He snapped his laptop closed. Okay, she was presenting a challenge, but he would win back control of the situation. "Chelsea, you will be paid well for doing this for me. If you insist, I will even agree to letting you leave your position early with full pay. That's one week of service as my assistant, or my nanny, or whatever you want to call it. And then you're done.

I get that it is above and beyond the call of duty; however, I will make it worth your while. Don't stress it. We'll drive there. I'll get to know my kid. You can play with rocks with her or whatever. This isn't a big deal."

She slapped her tablet onto the desk and, surprisingly, the screen didn't shatter at the force of the impact. Without a word, she spun on her heel to head for the door.

He was up before he really thought through the implications of running after her, but he managed to snag her arm before she could make it out the door. It struck him that he'd never actually touched his assistant before. Well, he was sure they'd shaken hands at some point when he'd hired her, but he never touched her since then. The feel of her arm in his hand sent sparks up to his wrist. This was *Chelsea*.

The woman he spent more time with than anyone else in his life, either personal or business. She was as close to a friend as he actually had, even if their relationship was strictly that of an employee and employer. Surely, she'd understand.

Then again, if someone had asked him yesterday if she wasn't satisfied with her job, he would've said they'd be together until she retired. Showed how much he knew…

"Look, I should've said that differently. I'm sorry."

He meant the words and wasn't entirely surprised when she tilted her head back to look at him. "This isn't my job. It never has been, and it certainly isn't now that I'm gone in two weeks. I'm doing it for you and Waverley."

How had he never noticed the delicate dance of freckles across her nose before? Her eyes, something he never paid much attention to previously, were a warm chocolate brown. She was close enough that he smelled a teasing bit of her perfume—something musky with hints of vanilla—and his pulse sped in a way that it shouldn't.

Not for his assistant.

But he only said, "I get that. Thank you. I just don't know

how to connect with her yet, and I think it will be easier if I have someone familiar..." The word wasn't quite right, but he shook his head. "With us. She likes you. I like you. Thank you for agreeing to come. When we get back, you can interview a couple of candidates, train one up, and I'll release you from employment without further argument. I'll get you a copy of the email when I send it to Margo with all the travel plans, okay?"

She gnawed her bottom lip, and his eyes traced over that tempting bit of flesh. If she were any other woman, he might kiss her to further coerce her to agree. But she was Chelsea, smart and savvy, and that kind of nonsense wouldn't work with her.

Not to mention how quickly she'd storm to HR to report him for harassment.

He released her arm and leaned on the door, putting him in closer proximity to that tantalizing perfume she was wearing. It reminded him of candy—something delicious and decadent that would melt in his mouth as he devoured it.

"I'll keep an eye out for the email, but I'll need the day before we leave off work for packing and preparing to be gone. I'll bring my laptop, so I can work remote while we're gone and—"

"No," he interrupted. That fire—that teasing sense of something below the calm waters of her gaze—erupted again in her expression. Some perverse part of him longed to frustrate her further, just to see if it would ignite into a full-blown conflagration. But he continued, "You can take the time off work. Consider it paid vacation, but it won't subtract from the days you have accumulated so far this year. Sound fair?"

She shrugged, and this close, she nearly brushed his chest with her arm. "Fine." She put her hand on the door handle and added, "I'm taking a long lunch. I'll be back later."

With that, she left his office and closed the door gently behind her.

He didn't know what he'd do without her. She kept so much of his life sane, was an integral part of his company. Yet, for a second, he kind of wished she wasn't his assistant. How interesting would it be to get to know her as a woman rather than as an employee? She was fascinating.

Then again, he was probably just seeking a distraction, any distraction, from the situation with Waverley and Margo, so better not to go down that path.

Better to do what he always did—focus on work. Plan how to best control the situation and make it all go in his favor.

For some reason, the thrill of finessing a situation escaped him, though. He chalked it up to lack of sleep and went back to his desk to get some things done before Chelsea returned from her lunch.

Chapter Four

CHELSEA

The racks of brightly colored clothes should've been a distraction, but all Chelsea could think about was the fact that, in a few short hours, she'd be sleeping under the same roof as Aiden Kelley, her boss at Kelley Enterprises.

And one of the most notorious billionaires in the country, if not the world. The man was sex on legs, yet she was supposed to "consider it a severance vacation"—per his orders—and enjoy a trip with him and his daughter. Life really didn't get more surreal than what she faced right that second.

And the worst part? She couldn't even tell anyone it was happening. If the media got wind of this trip, their every step would be dogged by photographers. Not a big deal for her, but she guessed neither Margo Welles nor Aiden would want pictures of their daughter splattered over the headlines. Especially since Margo had apparently managed to keep the girl pretty hidden for this long... Aiden couldn't afford for her to become the focus of the paparazzi on his first visit.

So Chelsea couldn't say a word. Even if it was killing her and the only thing she wanted to do was spill all of it to her best friend Kimmie. Then she could ask her what she would do, how she would handle it, and maybe get some advice. Any advice, really, at this point would be welcome.

Kimmie held up a cute flowered tank top. "How about this?"

Although she loved it, the pattern was too much. She considered herself a simple woman, wearing mostly muted colors, and technically this was a work trip. A weird work trip, and her last, but still...a work trip no less.

"Nah, stick with more muted stuff." Chelsea halfheartedly picked up a pair of jeans. It was too bad, really, that she had no clue what sort of clothes to pack. Would he want to go out to nice restaurants in the evening? If so, she would need to pack something more formal...however, the fact that he had his magic kid—*just add sperm!*—on the trip implied he would not want to risk being recognized by going to any place his peers might be visiting. So probably casual stuff...?

If he intended for Waverley to get to see the rocks she wanted and be outdoors, she would need casual clothes, appropriate for walking around, but formal enough to show she was the employee and not on vacation herself.

But did it even matter what she wore? If the media did, for some reason, find out they were on this trip, then it wasn't likely they'd pay her much mind anyway. There were literally dozens of newspaper and magazine articles she'd saved over the years to send back to her dad, all of which only featured her arm or her leg or some other hardly recognizable portion of her anatomy. Most worked to crop her out of the shot because, at the end of the day, she was nothing more than the help. Invisible, until her employer needed her for something.

She liked to pretty it up, to consider herself important to him and to the Kelley empire, but realistically, she was the elbow in the background of the picture, not the focus.

"Are you ever going to explain what we're shopping for? It would be way easier to help you find whatever the hell you're looking for if I knew what that was." Kimmie's lips went tight and white, an outward sign of her annoyance.

"If I knew what to expect, I'd probably have an easier time telling you what to look for," Chelsea confessed.

"So you're going to…"

"The Grand Canyon," Chelsea finished.

"And you're going with…"

"It's for work," she answered with a small glare.

"With your sexy boss?" Kimmie pressed. Her russet eyes looked particularly dark in the florescent light, gleaming like dark jewels in the warm brown of her skin. "You're going on a spur-of-the-moment trip to the Grand Canyon with *the* Aiden Kelley."

Chelsea shrugged, not wanting to make it seem like a bigger deal than it was. She traveled with Aiden all the time. There was nothing, at least from the outside, which was particularly odd about that. "Yeah, I'm traveling with my boss for work. As one does."

"As one does, my ass." Kimmie snagged a cute little pleated skirt in a lovely slate gray off the rack. "You need this. That said, where are you guys staying?"

"I don't know," she confessed.

"For how long?"

"Not sure." She shifted from foot to foot before grabbing the skirt and a couple of other items and heading for the dressing rooms.

"Who all is going? Is Lucy going?" Kimmie wasn't a big Lucy fan.

"No, from my office, it is just me and Aiden." She closed the door in Kimmie's face, hoping she wouldn't overthink it. "Don't make a big deal out of nothing. It isn't what you're thinking."

"How do you know what I'm thinking?" Kimmie asked before letting a garment sail over the door of the dressing room. "Try this on."

"This is lingerie." She looked at the hot pink teddy and rolled her eyes. "Also, this is the same color as the bra I found in my office."

"Which proves he likes that color. Try it on, just for giggles." Kimmie laughed outside the door, and Chelsea opened it to peek at her.

"I told you not to overthink this."

"Honey, you're the one who overthinks it. That man is fine. You never know what will happen. Two attractive people, one big canyon, quiet misty mornings, late starry nights..." Kimmie grinned and pointed at the lace in Chelsea's hand. "Skimpy hot pink thongs."

"You're impossible," Chelsea said, closing the door. She wasn't going to try the lingerie on.

But she did hold it up against her chest experimentally, considering her reflection in the dreaded three-way mirror. Kimmie always said that lingerie wasn't worn for a man; it was worn for yourself. It was worn closest to the skin to remind a woman that she was indeed that—a woman. It was supposed to make you feel good.

Somehow, she didn't think that wearing a garment that was way too close in color and general style to what she'd found strewn around her and Aiden's office would make her feel good about herself or even a little sexy. It would make her feel inadequate. Her boobs wouldn't fill it out, it would be scratchy, and all in all not her idea of undergarments.

Not that she could feel sexy with him. He was her boss. At least, for now he was.

But still...

Nope, not her thing. She tossed it into the pile and tried

on the little skirt. It swung around her legs in a feminine way, and she had the naughty thought that it was long enough to cover her ass nicely.

If she were feeling sexy, she wasn't the sexy underwear type. She was more the no underwear—*surprise!*—kind of gal. There was something infinitely hot about the shocked look a man got on his face when he finally got his hand under her skirt and realized there was no barrier there.

She couldn't confess that to Kimmie—although it would probably crack her up and make her slap her on the shoulder before saying something like, "Ya nasty, but I love you."

She got back into her clothes, snagged the items she planned to buy, and then tucked the lingerie into the stack of items she didn't want. She kind of hid it in the pile, not wanting anyone to see that she'd even had it in the dressing room. She wasn't sure why the idea embarrassed her—especially after she'd decided to buy the skirt she'd imagined wearing without undergarments—but it did.

"You're no fun," Kimmie said, grumbling when she saw the lingerie wasn't in the keep pile. "You could at least mess with the man's mind."

"Trust me, the last thing Aiden Kelley needs is for me to mess with his mind. He has enough going on without it."

Kimmie squinted at her. "There is something else going on. And I'm getting that you can't tell me whatever it is."

"I can't," Chelsea agreed.

"But I don't need to know it to give you a little advice."

Kimmie went silent as Chelsea paid for her purchases and waited for the cashier to bag them up. Once they were back in the main hallway of the mall, though, she directed Chelsea over to a bench. Facing her, she took both her hands in her own.

"You can't tell me about whatever it is, but like I said, I have some advice."

"Advise away, oh wise one." Chelsea glanced across the hall and said, "Then I'll buy you a coffee."

"I'll take you up on that. Okay, I want you to remember one thing on this trip, the most important thing. You are valuable. You deserve love. He's not better than you; he's richer than you. At the end of the day, Aiden Kelley is just a person and so, if something happens…"

Chelsea rolled her eyes. "Nothing is going to happen." Even if, for just a second, it had felt like something weighted the air between her and Aiden for a moment there.

Even if part of her was so damn curious about what his lips would feel like against her own.

"Fine. If nothing happens, then I wasted five minutes of your time. But promise me you'll remember that. Because I think you're freaking awesome, and I wish you could see yourself the way I see you." Kimmie stared her down until Chelsea misted up a little.

"Got it. I'm special. And I love you, Kimmie."

They hugged and then headed over toward the coffee, but Chelsea didn't blow off her friend's words. Instead, she tried to let them soak in, to become part of what she believed about herself.

Not that it would matter, but still…

Chapter Five

Chelsea

The car wasn't a car at all. It was clearly an SUV, probably with extra features like security glass and who knew what else. Chelsea wasn't sure why she expected something else, but the black government-looking vehicle said nothing of the family road trips she remembered from her own childhood and a lot about cold, stuffy, sterile efficiency. Someone had already stowed their bags in the closed roof rack, and a man in a uniform held the door open as he waited for her to jump in the back. "We have a driver?" she asked. Another identical vehicle was parked behind them, full of what she assumed must be security. "And we're bringing security?"

She wasn't sure that she really expected Aiden to answer, but he spoke from too close behind her, jarring her senses and making her startle. "Of course we do. I can't drive."

Glancing at him over her shoulder, she raised one brow. "You can't drive, but you thought we should drive across country? Do you even know how to road trip?"

He shrugged, looking ruggedly but boyishly handsome in designer jeans and a white button-down shirt. "I've lived in cities my whole life. When I was a kid, I used public transport. When we visited the old country, I rode a bike, walked, or used the damnable buses that never are on time or don't stop to pick you up. Now? I have a driver. Never had a reason to learn, to be honest. Can you drive?"

Blinking at him, she tried to process all that. "The old country?"

With a laugh, he slung an arm across her shoulders. "Ireland, lass. Don't tell me you're not familiar with th' ol' country." He shook his head slowly, but the heavy accent on his words made her shiver. She had a thing for accents, most especially Irish ones. He might not know it, but he was really turning her on with that sexy way of talking.

"I know what Ireland is," she snapped, as if her being cranky would relieve the attraction his voice caused. "I've just never heard you call it that before."

"My parents crossed the pond before I was born, but the Irish…that's in the blood." He drawled the words, still using the damn accent, and tapped his chest near his heart. She only just barely resisted humping his leg.

"Whatever," she practically snarled. She didn't have a lot of defenses against Aiden's charms to begin with, but that voice could prove her downfall, which unreasonably annoyed her. "What time is Margo meeting us with Waverley?"

"We're picking her up along the way. Hop in," Aiden invited.

She got in the car and, in seconds it seemed, the driver managed to navigate the busy city streets and bring them to the door of one of the more posh apartment complexes. Rumor had it that rent in this building was somewhere around twelve thousand a month.

No wonder she wanted more money.

"I'll wait in the car," Chelsea offered.

"No," Aiden said quickly. "You should come with me."

Chelsea berated herself for agreeing to go on this trip. So she couldn't really afford to pay a penalty for quitting right now... Surely, there was another way than this? She called herself any number of names while she followed him to the shining doors held open by a uniformed doorman and again while entering the brass and stone decorated elevator. She continued to bash everything from her intelligence to her emotional fortitude as she tried to stay a few feet behind Aiden in the hallway, hoping maybe he'd talk to Margo, get his kid, and forget she was loitering somewhere behind him.

Instead, when Margo opened the door to her apartment, she waved them both inside. "I sent down her things a little while ago, and I talked to Hugo downstairs. He and your driver are loading them into the car. Why don't you both come in for a minute? Waverley!" The last was called out in a louder tone, meant to carry past the elegant entryway to her daughter somewhere nearby.

Margo Wells looked glamorous, even for so early in the day. Her silken red waves fell in careless abandon around the perfect oval of her lovely face, and her lush lips curved into the signature smile which had likely earned her millions over the years. "You must be Chelsea," she added, stretching a hand toward Chelsea. "Waverley has been talking nonstop about you. It's great to get a chance to really meet you."

Chelsea took Margo's delicate palm into her own and shook probably too vigorously, but the sheer perfection of the model turned mother made her feel like a ham-fisted ogre. "Pleasure to meet you as well, Ms. Wells," Chelsea managed.

"Thanks so much for giving me this chance with her," Aiden said, and Chelsea took his words as an opportunity to back up discreetly. She'd hide behind the potted palm at the door if she could.

"You made valid points. How could I say no?" The model's smile never wavered, but her tone seemed arctic cold. She didn't reach out to shake Aiden's hand or otherwise indicate she wanted to move any closer to him at all. Her body language was hard to read—open enough to suggest she was being friendly, yet closed off enough to suggest she didn't want to pretend to be chummy with Aiden.

But from Chelsea's perspective, they did make a striking pair. Her vivid hair looked even more radiant next to his dark head. Their heights were close enough that she looked him right in the eye when they spoke, and Chelsea couldn't help thinking they would still make a fabulous power couple. With her looks and his money, they could do just about anything...

And wouldn't that be nice for their kid? If they ended up back together from this whole fiasco, they'd be the most perfect little family and could buy a perfect house and maybe even get a perfect dog.

She chastised herself again for her bitter thoughts, but it was a damn good and timely reminder. No matter how sexy the accent might be, no matter how attractive her boss was, no matter how much he might seem like her friend sometimes... he wasn't. He was her boss, and people like them lived very different lives than anything Chelsea could hope for or dream about.

Then again, that she had to remind herself at all was probably a sign she should not go on this trip with him.

Waverley skidded to a sliding stop on the smooth, polished floor. Her socks were mismatched, her hair neatly braided, and her nose was scrunched as she looked up at her dad. "You could still back out. You know that, right?"

"Why would I want to back out?" asked Aiden, but he looked a little green around the gills, even to Chelsea.

"Last chance, Daddy wannabe," the child reiterated.

"Knock it off, Waverley," scolded her mother, and Chelsea

smiled for real.

They might be richer than she could comprehend, but at the end of the day…they were people. In an awkward situation.

And maybe she could help. Which was why she was here. "He's not backing down, kiddo. Your father is a stubborn man."

"And a control freak," added Margo. "Which means you're likely trouncing all over his schedule. Get your shoes on. Did you remember to pack your cell phone charger?"

Chelsea resisted snickering. When she was Waverley's age, she was thrilled to get a travel version of Connect Four. But the child got her shoes on, and in moments, they were loaded back into the sterile black SUV. Chelsea opted to sit in the front with the driver, leaving the back to Aiden and his child.

A full hour passed, during which she disobeyed Aiden's direct orders not to work and checked emails, messaged her family, and otherwise fiddled around with things on her phone. Her best friend Kimmie was among those who messaged her. *So did you chicken out, or are you in the car with Tony Stark right now?*

Chelsea snorted a half giggle, then got paranoid about Aiden seeing the message. A glance to the back seat showed both father and daughter plugged into chargers and engrossed in their own phones. *Way to bond*, she thought.

To Kimmie, she answered, *Yeah, I'm in the car now, but I can verify that the only power suits Aiden owns are not operated by battery nor can they change him into a super hero. I checked.*

Kimmie's answer beeped into her phone seconds later. *So…is he being a dicknugget, or is he being charming?*

Twisting her lips into a grimace, she snuck another peek behind her before responding. *Neither. He's being my boss, and this is a job, and that's all there is to it. He's been nothing but polite. I'm being well compensated for this; I get to go see the Grand Canyon for free. Nothing more, nothing less.*

Ha! Kimmy responded. *Are you kissing his ass because he's reading over your shoulder or what?*

The sound of Aiden's seatbelt unclicking was followed by Aiden leaning forward in the seat to peer over her shoulder. "Why do you keep peeking back here with that guilty look on your face? Are you working or something?"

She stuffed her phone into her purse and glared at him. "You make me sound like a workaholic."

He smiled in a slow way that had her toes curling in her sensible flats. "You're the one that wore a power suit on vacation, Chels."

"I am still technically working," she reminded him.

His chuckle floated forward as he relaxed back into his seat and refastened his seatbelt.

• • •

AIDEN

Aiden snapped awake only to realize he shouldn't move. His daughter's small head leaned on his shoulder. She smelled, unexpectedly, like some odd combination of crayons and little girl sweetness… Then again, perhaps that was what a daughter smelled like. It wasn't like he had any room for comparison.

What had she been like as a baby? How old was she when she learned to walk? What was her first word?

Had she ever wondered about him?

As he scrubbed a hand across his face, it occurred to him that he didn't know what woke him up. He could see the back of Chelsea's head well enough to tell that she'd also dozed off, leaning against the glass of the passenger side window. The driver, though…

Where was the driver? And why were they parked? Fears of kidnappings and ransoms danced in his paranoid head like unwelcome sugarplums.

The sun still beamed down from outside, so he carefully moved Waverley until she rested against the seat so he could look around and figure out what was going on.

The view outside his window wasn't the city at all. Heavy flowerpots hung from streetlamps, and green grass stretched out in front of what looked to be a town hall. A hand-painted sign on the lawn proclaimed they were throwing their 75th Annual County Strawberry Festival in the depot village, whatever that meant. On the other side of the road, he could see a gas station next to what looked like a diner right off a movie set.

"Where are we?" Chelsea asked, twisting around to face him from the front seat. Apparently, while he'd been considering the view and wondering the same thing, she'd awakened with the same confusion.

"I don't know," Aiden answered honestly, but then he spotted his driver coming out of the gas station. He weaved a bit, looking not well whatsoever, yet he made his way back to the car. "You okay, Jimmy?" he asked the driver once he'd taken his seat behind the wheel.

"No, actually," Jimmy admitted. He met Aiden's eyes in the rearview mirror. "Migraine."

The one-word explanation caused ice to skitter over Aiden's skin. His pulse thumped in his ears, and he could feel his hands beginning to shake, so he fisted them in his lap. Jimmy's eyes looked a little puffy and bloodshot, meaning the man was telling the truth, but that left them stranded.

Him, Waverley, and Chelsea, stranded who knew where? His heart raced, and it felt like someone had placed a lead weight on his chest.

Get it together.

He was the Irish Prince. He'd built a company from scratch, stood up against fierce competitors, and come out ahead of them all.

Nothing bad would happen. He could call…

Who exactly could he call to fix this? He didn't even know where they were. If he'd just taken the plane…

Chelsea's hand landed on his knee, oddly comforting, although he should be the one making things easier for her. After all, she hadn't even wanted to go on this trip.

"Are you okay?" Chelsea said.

"I'm fine."

She raised an eyebrow. "Because you look a little panicked."

"I don't get panicked."

"Okay. But you get anxious in situations where you haven't planned everything down to the last detail. And you didn't exactly plan on being stranded here with your daughter."

He looked back at Waverley, the pinch of panic tightening a little. How had she noticed? He made a point of keeping his anxiety carefully hidden, and this wasn't the first time she'd hinted she recognized his unwelcome reaction to situations outside the realm of his control. "Exactly why I can't afford to be panicked."

"Okay. Where are we, Jimmy?" she asked the driver. He'd closed his eyes and rested his head back on the seat, but he stirred and peered at her.

"Ohio. Some small town not far from the interstate. I needed to get some ibuprofen, sorry." Jimmy sounded truly apologetic, but it didn't tamp back on the lump rising in Aiden's throat.

A cop car pulled up alongside their vehicle. Waverley stirred, sat up, and blinked around. "Where are we?" she asked, sounding disoriented.

"Ohio," Chelsea answered, removing her hand from Aiden's knee. He felt the loss of it and was tempted to snatch her hand back. "Have you ever been to Ohio?"

"No..." The little girl elongated the o's at the end of the word, her wide eyes focused on the police car. "Are we pulled over?"

"Nope." Chelsea opened her door, letting more bright sunshine into the vehicle. Jimmy cringed, but Chelsea didn't look back inside, instead stretching her lovely little body out in the warm rays from above. "Looks like there is a parade coming through. C'mon, Waverley. Let's go check it out."

"But—" Aiden began. It wasn't safe. And where was the car with his security team?

Neither of the girls listened to him. Waverley popped out of the car, leaving her door hanging open, and Jimmy seemed to wither a bit more. Probably too much sunlight. Aiden remembered reading somewhere that light was bad for migraines.

"Hey, Jimmy, why don't you crawl into the back and shut your eyes for a while?" Chelsea said, peeking in her door. "It's darker back there. We'll go check out this parade and be back in a bit. Sound good?"

Aiden opened and closed his mouth like a fish. The panic still scraped at him, but he recognized his own weakness—he hated feeling out of control, as if by simply maneuvering the world around him, he kept sanity in place. Chelsea was breaking all the rules. One didn't just go roaming around a strange town in the armpit of America. "Chelsea, I think..."

She grinned back at him, taking Waverley's hand when the girl reached her side. "Oh, hush, Aiden. It'll be fun. Come on. Live a little."

He was way outside his element, in a situation beyond his control and in an unfamiliar place. He could see now that Chelsea had been right—some sort of parade was making its way down the broad country street—and likely his daughter would enjoy the experience.

But it was also a place of unfamiliar potential dangers. A really bad idea.

For Waverley, and all the years he'd missed with her, he'd try, though. "Yeah, Jimmy. Grab some shut eye, and we'll be back shortly."

"Thanks, boss," Jimmy said, while Aiden got out of the car and stepped into the unknown.

Chapter Six

Chelsea

She knew Aiden didn't do surprises well. Hell, he'd abolished company surprise parties, even in cases of birthdays and retirements, not because he didn't like them socializing...but because he hated disorder.

After working with him for so many years, she'd realized that what others mistook as him being a control freak was something else entirely. The man might be wealthy, powerful, and sometimes even feared—but he freaked out when he was off his precious schedules. She wasn't a doctor, so she couldn't begin to try to label what was off about Aiden Kelley, but she could recognize it and had in the past found ways to make some things easier for him and those around him.

For instance, a surprise party was fine, so long as the surprise wasn't on Aiden—she had to warn him in advance so he could plan it into his day. Just about anything, in fact, was fine, so long as it was in his schedule.

This trip? She knew he'd planned most of it down to the

hour. Impulsive and spontaneous were two words he was practically allergic to, so this little stop in small town Ohio? Had to have him near panicked.

Which was why she'd reached out to touch him. Funny thing, that…no one ever seemed to touch Aiden. Well, other than the women he dated, but that was hardly a touch intended to inspire comfort. He lived in this bubble of his own superior-ness, and few felt comfortable enough with him to do more than shake his hand.

But Waverley showed none of her father's reticence at the impulsive. The little girl was alight with excitement. So far, she'd collected candy off the street when the firefighters threw it from their place in the parade, managed to make friends with a little girl in a princess dress, and danced when the marching band went by. While her father, looking stoic and worried, stood a few feet back—well on the curb—with his hands stuffed in his pockets and a dark expression on his handsome face.

She stepped back to join him and was able to hear Aiden's soft words, clearly intended for her ears only. "I hope you're not planning to let her eat that candy. They threw it on the road. The same road those horses are using for a toilet over there."

Hc gestured with his shoulder, and Chelsea bit back a giggle. "Five-second rule?" she tried.

Her boss glared at her. "I can call back to the city, have the service send me another driver. I have no clue how we lost the car load of security, but likely they're stopped behind this parade somewhere. I'm sorry that this happened. I should've had a backup plan."

From Chelsea's perspective, that would've been a terrible idea. "Sometimes, in life, we are better off working without a plan. I can drive."

She waited, watching Waverley as she grabbed more candy,

this time thrown from a float covered in local cheerleaders. Her father cringed as she unwrapped a sucker and popped it into her mouth without the slightest hesitation. "I could've bought her candy if she'd wanted it," he said, ignoring her offer to drive. "I know of some great gourmet chocolatiers and candy makers back in the city."

Chelsea didn't bother to resist the eye roll that his words evoked. "Dude, seriously...she's a kid, not one of your paramours. She likely prefers that candy to anything you could've bought her. Besides, she's having fun."

He grunted. She took that to mean he couldn't disagree to the fun but wasn't thrilled with Chelsea right that second. She reiterated, "I can drive, Aiden."

"Don't be ridiculous," he practically snarled. One of his hands came out of his pocket briefly, reaching out as if to stop Waverley, who'd bounced back into the road to pick up more candy. But the child was clearly safe, and the little girl in the princess dress was by her side as they each accepted a balloon from a clown in the parade. His hand went back into his pocket, and he didn't say anything more.

"Look." She turned to face him head on so that she knew he had her attention. "The pamphlet says there are rides, fun, games, and food at the Strawberry Festival. When this parade is over, I vote that we walk over there," she pointed in the general direction that the signs indicated led to the depot where the festival was to take place, "and have a fun little distracting day. No one knows who we are here. Security will just draw attention, and then someone might recognize us, so this is a unique opportunity. Waverley will have a blast, it will give Jimmy time to recover if you don't want me to drive, and we'll be back on the road in no time. Sure, we'll lose part of a day of travel time, but according to your itinerary..."

She tried not to sound as disgusted by the itinerary as she felt, but none of her family trips included a schedule. Planning time like that didn't allow for any fun, in her opinion, but it wasn't her place to argue with him. Only to help him make the best of what was going on, help him bond with his kid, then go back to her normal life at the end of this fiasco.

"I'm not obsessed with my schedule," he asserted, looking down his nose at her.

This time, she resisted rolling her eyes, but it was a real struggle. "I never said you were."

"But you think I am. You think I can't just have fun, roll with the punches, be spontaneous," he accused.

No, she didn't think that… She *knew* it. Well, unless it involved "entertaining" in her office. He managed spontaneity then, apparently. "I didn't say you couldn't be spontaneous, either," she pointed out.

"Can we go with Mabel over to the festival?" Waverley asked. The cop cars were moving, freeing the street up to traffic again. Both girls—the princess and Waverley—were holding hands, and a woman stood nearby, jiggling a baby on her shoulder. Chelsea would guess she was the mother of the princess.

Chelsea didn't answer Waverley, instead looking at Aiden expectantly. She could try to loosen him up, but she couldn't force him. After all, at the end of the day…he was the boss. Even if he was entirely out of his element and adorably frustrated by exactly that.

"Sounds like fun, Waverley," her father said. His hands were still stuffed in his pockets, and his shoulders were tight with tension. Chelsea could see that he was vastly uncomfortable, but he was trying.

Sometimes, people didn't have to be perfect, in Chelsea's opinion. They just had to be trying.

"We were thinking of staying for lunch and some rides… Does that sound fun to you?" he asked the little girl, following close on the heels of his daughter and her princess friend.

"Yes, thanks!" Waverley practically bounced, her red hair gleaming in the sunshine, and her father looked like some angry guardian as he kept close on the walk toward the depot.

Chelsea smiled at them both. Maybe they'd be able to make this whole thing work, after all.

• • •

AIDEN

Scratching at his neck, Aiden watched his daughter as she climbed the rickety-looking staircase to the top of the bright yellow, plastic slide. Once she'd mounted the dangerous-looking structure, a worker handed her a burlap sack and helped her get into position to ride the steep slide. The child's laughter pleased him, but none of it would've happened without Chelsea.

Glancing at the woman in question, he saw her head bent over her phone. Although it was likely a violation of her privacy, he took advantage of his greater height and peered over her shoulder.

Annoyance flared, making his neck itch even more than it had moments before. "Really, Chelsea? I thought I said no work during this trip."

Her brown eyes were wide when she glanced up at him. He recognized her guilty expression but was more amused than annoyed. Not that he planned to reveal that to her.

"You did," she agreed. He saw her click send before stuffing the phone back in her purse. She might feel guilty about getting caught, but it didn't stop her from working anyway. "But since you hired me to come with you, I can't *not* work, now can I?"

Her triumphant smile said she'd thought she managed a neat bit of circular reasoning, but he wasn't letting it go. He scratched his wrist and nodded toward the lemonade stand.

"Need another drink?" he offered.

"Thanks, but no," she answered. Her smile got bigger as Waverley hopped off the sack at the bottom of the slide and rejoined them. "Having fun, kiddo?"

"Sure am! Uh, is his face supposed to look like that?" Waverley peered up at him, her expression a bit worried.

"Like what?" Chelsea asked before she, too, stared at Aiden. "Oh, dear..."

"What?" he asked. He resisted scratching his neck again, but it was a battle. Maybe he was allergic to country life.

Chelsea's eyes widened. "Aiden, do you have any food allergies that I don't know about?"

"I..." He glanced around. "Strawberries, but just being around them shouldn't bother me."

"No." Chelsea caught his wrist and tugged him to follow her. "But eating them probably is a dumbass idea."

"I didn't eat any strawberries," he pointed out. Although Waverley and Chelsea had enjoyed what looked like a delicious strawberry shortcake in the old rail station portion of the historic depot village, he'd abstained.

"The lemonade," Chelsea said.

"Ah," said Waverley.

"What?" he asked. "Lemonade has lemons, not strawberries."

He allowed her to tug him but mostly because the itching was distracting.

The look Chelsea narrowed on him was annoyed past frustration. "It was pink," she pointed out.

"So?" He'd had pink lemonade before. No problem.

"Pink because they had strawberries in it, you goon." He might have complained at her choice of words, but she looked genuinely worried. Chelsea stopped at one of the booths, one selling a bunch of handmade soaps, and he considered them. Yeah, he had a food allergy, but how bad could it really be?

He hadn't had strawberries since he was a kid, but he wasn't that concerned.

"Is there an ambulance parked on the grounds?" she asked the soap maker.

"I don't need an ambulance, Chels," he explained. "Sorry," added for the soap maker's benefit.

"Wow. Yeah, right over there. Behind the corn dog station. Is he okay?" asked the soap maker.

"Are you okay?" Waverley looked worried.

"I'm fine," he assured her.

"He's not fine," Chelsea said. She proceeded to haul him to the ambulance in question, and he went mostly because Waverley still seemed concerned.

A glance in the reflective surface on the side of the ambulance hiked his own worries through the roof. "What the hell?"

"Language," chastised Chelsea. "Hey, can you help me out?"

The EMT caught one look at Aiden and said, "Allergic reaction?"

"Yeah," Chelsea sighed. "Apparently, it didn't occur to him that pink lemonade would have strawberries in it."

Some allergy medicine and time on the stretcher later—although Aiden still thought they were blowing the whole thing out of proportion—he groggily itched his way behind the ladies. Waverley still bounced, talking a mile a minute to Chelsea, who kept glancing back at him, concern keeping her elegant brows low over her eyes. He wanted to grumble at her, tell her for the millionth time he was fine, but he could tell it would be a practice in futility.

One thing Aiden hated most—futility.

After a brief conversation with Jimmy, Chelsea rounded on him again. The damn medicine made him sleepy, but he put forth an effort to concentrate on the annoyed oval of her lovely face. "You're well and truly doped up, aren't you?"

"At least the anxiety backed off a bit," he admitted. Then he rubbed a hand over his face. He hadn't meant to admit to that. "I'm fine," he said instead, not altogether positive if he'd verbalized the first bit or just thought he did.

Chelsea sighed. "Jimmy still has a migraine, and I got an email back from Kimberly at the office—"

"I told you not to work," he said. Or whined. He was very irritated to realize his voice sounded whiney rather than commanding.

"She is going to send someone to pick up Jimmy. I managed to book him a night at the B&B for him to use while he waits for them to show up. I think I should drive. Apparently, security took a wrong exit, and they're still working their way back toward us." Chelsea looked particularly stubborn, which annoyed him to no end.

"I don't pay you to be a driver, Chels." He figured that was a mostly reasonable response. "Besides, they have to spend years learning how to do the map reading and the driver-ing. You have no skills in that area."

Her face said he hadn't sounded nearly as practical as he'd hoped. "Actually, I have maps on my phone and have always had my license. I can handle this. Why don't you go stretch out in the back seat and *let* me handle this?"

He opened his mouth to argue, but it came out a yawn. "Fine, I'll obey you but only because I need a minute to collect myself."

"Collect away," she said. If he wasn't mistaken, she snickered.

Chapter Seven

Aiden

He awoke to giggles. Not creepy ones, but his daughter happily laughing as she pointed out her window. "Thought you said no one ever found Alaska? I just found one."

Out the window, the world blurred by at a fast clip. In the dark, he couldn't see a lot, but he recognized a lot of corn. "Where are we?" he asked.

"Ah, sleeping beauty woke up," Chelsea said, her tone a warm balm to his still-a-little-jangled nerves. He wasn't used to sleeping in vehicles, and the view out his window was so foreign from what he was accustomed to, it just left him feeling out of place.

"He's not sleeping beauty. He's a boy," Waverley said, still chuckling. "New York!"

"You're really stomping me at this game, kiddo," Chelsea answered.

"What game?" he asked, rubbing his face and trying to force himself awake.

Waverley peeked back at him, twisting in her seat a bit to get a better view. "The license plate game. Have you ever played it?"

Games weren't really his thing, never had been. He was too competitive and rarely saw the fun in them. But based on the clear happiness on his child's face, he might have to learn to look at them in a new way. "Nope. Want to teach me?"

Waverley rolled her eyes. "You're super old, even older than Chelsea, but you don't already know how?"

"Hey," he grumbled. "Who said I was old?"

Chelsea's answering laughter wrapped him in sudden and completely unexpected carnal need. He worked to control the unwanted response as she spoke. "I told her you were older than me. She asked. Not my fault. And you are a couple years older. Hey, there's a gas station up ahead, and we can fuel up there. We can even get your dad some coffee, so he can wake up a bit more from the meds. Sound good?"

"Sure! I have to go to the restroom anyway," Waverley said.

Although the idea of gas station coffee didn't really appeal, stretching his legs did. He felt like every muscle in his body had tightened to a knot. Once Chelsea parked the car, he unwound and stretched. He obediently followed the ladies to the bathrooms and then followed them back outside before his brain really started working again.

"You know how to pump gas?" he asked Chelsea. Waverley had gotten back into the car and was blasting some sugary pop music so loud that the windows on the SUV rattled in complaint. Chelsea wasn't really paying attention to him, either. She instead inserted a card in the pump and then deftly popped the handle into the side of the vehicle.

"Yup, I sure do. You hired a very multi-talented executive assistant, boss man." Her somewhat cockeyed smile reminded him of his earlier moments of attraction toward her, and perhaps impulsively, he stepped closer to her to brush a lock of hair back from her forehead.

This close, he could smell her. He could see the way her pupils dilated when he touched her. He could hear the quick intake of breath as she otherwise went very, very still.

"I can't begin to thank you enough for your quick thinking and willingness to help make all of these bumps in the road smooth for Waverley," he said.

But what he was thinking was that kissing her might not be such a bad idea after all. He was thinking of how her lips might taste and how she'd fit into his arms.

"Glermpfh," she answered, turning away.

Faced with her stiff and poised back, he considered that response. She'd moved to stare at the pump as the numbers ticked upward, but her hand shook.

Just a little. Not something he even would've noticed if he hadn't been so intently studying her. "We should get a room," he said.

She abruptly yanked the nozzle out of the car but didn't stop squeezing the handle, sloshing gas all over the side of the car and onto his legs and shoes. Her scent vanished, washed away in the noxious fumes of fuel. "Ugh!" she sputtered. "What the hell are you talking about?"

"You just sprayed me with gasoline," he pointed out, surprised at how calm he sounded. The shoes were one of his favorite pairs, and he figured they were ruined. "And you're asking me what I'm talking about?"

"You said get a room," she practically shrieked at him. She grabbed globs of paper towels from a dispenser near the pump and mopped up the side of the car before scrubbing them against his legs and feet. Not once did she bother to look up at him, but she continued to rant. "What am I even supposed to think when you say something like that? Nothing. I can't think anything when my boss, which, yes—hello! You're still my boss. You should not be saying things like that to me. What are you thinking?"

Amused beyond words, even though he was still covered in gas—and now bits of paper towel as the delicate paper was leaving tiny globs all over his jeans—he reached down and caught her wrist. Pulling her up so they were again face to face, he said softly, "For the night. We should get a room for the night and start out again in the morning. All of us—me, you, and Waverley."

Although, now that she mentioned it, getting a room with her would be a hell of a lot of fun. He liked that her mind had also strayed that direction, even if she quickly got back on track and remembered that at least for the remainder of this trip, she was still his employee.

"Oh." She sniffed once and then looked at the paper towels in her hands. "Of course you meant that."

She discarded the handful into a nearby trash receptacle before glancing at him again. "Look, I'm sorry. I have no idea why I made that leap of assumption. You're right. We should get a room. Today has been...chaotic, so I apologize for my mistake and the gas thing."

"No apologies needed." Especially since his mind had been in the very same gutter. "Not to mention, you're going to be stuck inhaling these fumes until we do find a place for the night. Let me give Gary back at the office a call, and we'll see what is nearby in the way of lodgings."

He turned and walked away from her but couldn't resist one final glance back. Scolding himself mentally, he forced his thoughts back to what would be in the best interest of Waverley. Not her father seducing his executive assistant—that needed to stay at the top of the list.

Besides, in a few short weeks, Chelsea would be gone. No sense getting attached to her on yet another level just to lose her when she quit. It wasn't like he'd see her around—without the work they shared, he'd likely never see her again.

The thought was like a weight in his stomach.

Then again, maybe that was just the reason to give into his cravings when it came to her. There wouldn't be any consequences if she didn't work for him anymore—fulfill his craving and move on with his life. Funny thing was the more time he spent with her out of the office, the less earth shattering the idea of hooking up with Chelsea seemed. And the less he could imagine going on without her when she left.

• • •

CHELSEA

Chelsea reminded herself he was doped up on so much Benadryl, he probably wouldn't remember any of it. Well, the gas. He'd probably recall that one time she sprayed him with gasoline like she was planning his eminent and fiery end.

But *maybe* not.

She might have gotten lucky. They'd gotten lucky so far—the little festival in the town was a great day, at least until he'd had his allergic reaction. But they'd fixed that and gotten back on the road with no problems, other than the driver's migraine. Aiden hadn't had any other ill effects, and the medicine seemed to have fixed his allergy issue—even if he did itch a bit when they were checking in. The gas station moment, although embarrassing beyond belief, wasn't even a problem, really.

She was sure a shower and a change of clothes probably erased all evidence of her massive mistake. Probably.

Who was she kidding? This trip had been an utter disaster so far, and they'd not even made it to the official halfway point of the trip. She was a damn good assistant. So far, she'd sucked donkey nuggets at being a good road trip companion.

What had she been thinking, anyway? When he'd said

"get a room," he might have meant it as a euphemism for sex? Ha! She'd been projecting; that was what happened. She found him attractive, so she was stupid enough to project her own attraction onto him. He'd been standing there, still doped up from allergy meds, and she'd assumed he was coming on to her.

Just because the man flat-out did it for her, ringing all her bells and whistles so to speak, didn't mean he was attracted back. Not to mention how wildly inappropriate it would be if he did ever notice she was, well, female. Not that he would, since she wasn't an actress or a model or otherwise even moderately what he'd marked as his type again and again.

She hesitated at the door, trying to work up the bravery to cross into the shared room of the posh suite Gary managed to finagle based on their location when Aiden called him the night before. Hell, just looking around the room she'd been given, she should realize logically that there was no way a man like Aiden Kelley would be interested in a woman like her. The room rate for this place was likely more than her yearly salary.

Sighing, she decided to stop second guessing everything and just turn the damn knob. It wasn't like she could hide in her room until the whole trip was over and not face him ever again. He was her boss, she had a job to do, and she needed to put on her big girl—not gas-soaked—panties and go deal with it.

Even if part of her still insisted that they'd been having a moment at that gas pump. Even if she would swear on her grave that for a second—brief as it might have been—she'd felt an answering attraction from him and fantasized that he might bend down and kiss her.

In front of his kid, no less. Sure, Waverley hadn't been paying attention to them but…

There was no way he was attracted to her. End of story.

She'd sprayed him with gasoline, anyway, so even if the lust-fueled part of her brain insisted otherwise, there was no way that she hadn't doused the possibility with her actions.

Sick of being alone with her own circular thoughts, she opened the door and faced her doom.

But there was no doom awaiting her on the other side of the door. Just Waverley, looking adorable and a little lost in the posh living room area. The child held a hairbrush in one hand and chewed her lip. The other arm was hugging what looked like a very battered blue-and-white bear so tight to her chest, the poor thing would be strangled if it were alive.

"Hey, kiddo. Good morning!" Smiling at Waverley, she moved to join her. "You're looking a little lost. What's up?"

"My mom usually braids my hair. Even if we're traveling, she says it is our girly time, and she does my hair every single morning. Guess I'm missing her a little." Waverley's lip trembled in a way that had every maternal instinct Chelsea never knew she had screaming in protest.

"Well, I'm sure your dad can learn how to do that for when you're visiting, but for right now, would you like me to do it?" She held out a hand for the brush.

Waverley passed it to her, looking relieved. "I mean, I could do it myself, but…"

"But you're missing your mom. I get it. You guys are close?" Deftly, she split the little girl's soft hair down the middle and twisted one side into a band that the child offered. It wasn't much different than doing her doll's hair when she was a kid, which was surprisingly nostalgic for Chelsea.

"Yeah, I guess. Isn't everyone close to their mom?" Waverley started to turn, but Chelsea moved with her so she didn't lose the hair she had begun braiding. Also, she didn't really want to meet her eyes, fearing her own might give away pain she didn't want to share with a child.

"I suppose. I was raised by my father, though, so I don't

personally have that kind of experience." She kept her tone modulated, not sad, which wasn't too hard. She didn't remember much of her mother, so there wasn't a lot of loss to mourn.

Or so she reminded herself on the rare moment when she got sad thinking of what might have been if life worked out differently.

"Really?" Waverley sounded amazed. Not surprising, since single mothers were quite common, while single fathers weren't as talked about, in Chelsea's experience. "Who did your hair? Taught you stuff? Like, how does that even work?"

Finishing off the first braid, Chelsea tied it off with a band before moving to the other side. "Probably the same way it works for single mothers raising sons. He learned what he needed to know so he could take care of me. He used to braid my hair, just like I'm doing yours. He'd polish my nails. Oh, and every morning, he'd sing me this little ditty…" Chelsea laughed, just thinking about it.

"A ditty? What is that?" Waverley sounded confused.

"A song. He'd sing, 'Good morning, morning glory, and how are you today? It's such a pretty morning, it's time for us to sa-a-ay… Good morning, morning glory, and how are you today!' Silly, but it still makes me happy." Tying off the second braid, she allowed Waverley to face her.

"Do you think my dad will be like that?"

The child's simple question was made all the more poignant by the fact that Chelsea could see Aiden enter the room out of the corner of her eye—just in time to hear his daughter's question and appear a little stunned.

"I'm sure, if you give him time, he could be even better than my dad was," Chelsea answered, glancing up to see Aiden's surprise at her faith in him.

Chapter Eight

Chelsea

Since he hadn't brought up her inability to control a gas pump on the remainder of their drive to the Grand Canyon, she didn't, either. She'd taught them the license plate game and a few old camp songs she remembered from her childhood.

When Chelsea asked him if he remembered any songs from his camping days—sure he'd probably went to some rich kid camp or something, and she didn't know whether or not they even sang like regular kid camps—he surprised her by saying his parents were never able to afford that kind of thing.

She tried to imagine him as anything other than the rich and powerful man she worked for but came up with nothing. He was Aiden Kelley, billionaire, and the press loved him. He had shiny toys, gorgeous women, and more power than he needed. He controlled people and things with bored grace. He wasn't like everyone else—like her. He was one of the elite.

But he insisted he'd come from a family which bordered

on poverty level his whole childhood. She tried to imagine him as a normal kid, with scruffy hair and missing teeth, but her brain refused to even cooperate. Somehow, she'd thought he was born with a silver spoon shoved firmly up his privileged ass.

So to further pass the time, she had him sync his phone to the car and they played Name That Tune, movie and television theme song version. Apparently, it had never occurred to him to even look up old theme songs, but he was laughing as hard as his daughter.

Aiden and his daughter not only looked alike, it turned out they shared a love of comic books—another facet of his personality she never would've guessed at. "I worked summers bagging groceries and delivering papers," he admitted. "Saved every spare dime to buy comics. Well, that and Whatchamacallit candy bars."

Which prompted a stop at a gas station so he could buy one for Waverley. She'd never tried one, which he thought was a travesty of her childhood so far. They munched them and talked comics—a conversation which left Chelsea lots of time for thinking, since she didn't know Captain Wonderwoman from Iron Spider, or whatever the hell their names were.

Basically, she kind of felt like a third wheel and tried to focus on just driving. Her being left out of the conversation, she reminded herself, was a very good thing, because it meant they didn't need her as a buffer. The whole point of this trip was for Aiden to connect with his daughter, and based on the conversation over the duration of the drive, it worked like a charm.

• • •

Once they'd gotten the key and checked into the gorgeous and no doubt overpriced cabin he'd rented for the week—

because why would he just get a hotel room like a normal person?—she'd done her best to fade into the shadows. Even after what should have been a good night's sleep in a plush and decadent bed, she was tired and cranky. Then again, she'd spent most of the night tossing and turning.

Chelsea stretched as she padded down the wide-plank, hand-hewn wooden floor of the hallway toward the central room of the cabin. It was nice not being on the road anymore. Her ass was still numb from being in the car for so long, and she secretly hoped he'd book a plane back. Although the ride had been fun at points, she'd be happy not to be in a car for at least another year or two.

She slammed to a stop when she got to the kitchen. If she'd thought he'd have a chef or some other set up for food, she'd been very, very wrong. Or at least she was wrong this morning, or he'd gotten some wild hair up his ass and decided to cook.

Because instead of a chef in the kitchen, a shirtless and barefoot Aiden stood over the stove, flipping pancakes to go with, based on scent, what was some delicious bacon. He hummed softly while he cooked, and if she were to guess... he was humming the theme song to *The Greatest American Hero*.

If she hadn't already lusted after the man before, she would've started right that second.

Reminding herself of his cocky, bossy nature at work wasn't curing her crush. Thinking of the model who gave birth to his child wasn't dulling it. Everything in her wanted to walk up behind him and give him a hug.

Which was lame. If her imagination had ideas about him, shouldn't they be all about sweat-slicked skin and silk sheets? Not something simple like a hug. It seemed even her imagination was terrifically mundane, just like the rest of her.

She'd lingered in the doorway for too long, because he

turned and made her heart squeeze with his easy smile. "Good morning," he rumbled, his voice still a bit gruff from sleep.

Which annoyed her unreasonably. Apparently, he'd slept well and woken up in a great mood. While she'd been tossing and turning and overthinking everything, he'd probably snored the night away without a worry in the world. Without saying anything in response, she moved to the coffee pot to grab a cup of magical go-go juice.

"Sleep well?" he asked.

"Of course he's chipper in the morning. All smiles and bacon and smiling. Refreshed and looking as if he doesn't have a care in the world…he could at least look scruffy or have bags under his eyes like a normal human being. It just isn't right."

"Have I mentioned that your annoyed mumbling drives me crazy? Because it still drives me crazy," he said. The bastard had the audacity to smile while he said it, though, which only aggravated her further. She quit mumbling, all the same, not even realizing she'd started.

Once she had the mug poured, she doctored it with sugar and cream and took the first sip of life-giving, sanity-bringing caffeine. She focused on the warmth of the cup in her hand, in the smooth way each gulp went down, in the sweet aftertaste, and tried to ignore the nearly naked man practically dancing on his too-sexy feet as he continued to make breakfast and hum.

The *bastard*. It was downright dastardly of him to be so chipper and adorable so early in the day. The least he could do was be a jerk and remind her why wanting him was beyond stupid.

Once she'd finished the mug, she finally answered him. "Good morning."

"Not a morning person, huh? You always seem so personable in the office."

"Well, it certainly isn't gentlemanly of you to point it out. You're right, though. No talkie before the coffee." She smirked at her own joke and poured herself a second cup. At least he'd managed to get good coffee. She could live without a lot of things—sex, sanity, reasonable separation of work and home life—but she couldn't abide living without good coffee.

"When has anyone accused me of being a gentleman?" he asked with a devious grin.

She was saved from having to answer by Waverley joining them. Her red waves bounced around her grinning face as she plopped down at one of the hewn-log chairs. "Good morning, morning glory, and how are you today?" she chirped.

"It's such a pretty morning, it's time for us to sa-a-ay..." Chelsea replied. It would help if his kid was less awesome. A rock hound *and* she remembered Chelsea's dad's song? Yeah, the kid was too much.

"Good morning, morning glory, and how are you today!" Waverley finished. "Can we go see the canyon today?"

"I made pancakes," Aiden said, placing a plate loaded with more pancakes and bacon than any kid could eat in front of her. "Eat up."

"You didn't answer me. Are we going?" The child's smile dried up, and a frown furrowed her pretty little brow.

"Not today," Aiden began, holding up a hand to ask Waverley to let him finish his sentence.

Although that particular hand had and could halt just about any adult Chelsea ever met, Waverley was apparently made of sterner stuff. "The only reason I agreed to this trip with you was to see the Grand Canyon. And you brought me all this way, and you're not going to take me? I'm going to call my mom."

Her words made Chelsea frown. Emotional blackmail, apparently, was a skill kids learned early these days.

"You can call her if you want; however, I'm your father,

and I said we aren't going today." Aiden glanced at Chelsea as if to see if she disapproved or not, but she decided to let them work it out. She simply sipped her coffee and waited. "We've been on the road for a couple days, and I don't know about you, but I have no desire to get back in a car today. I know we're in the Canyon and it is close, but there is a pool out back and lots of rocks around the cabin. I vote we stay here for the day."

Waverley shrugged, not looking happy about it, but she tucked into the pancakes before saying anything more. When she finally did speak after the first bite, she squinted at her dad. "We're just going to hang out in a cabin all day? Sounds boring. Also, how come you can cook, but my mom can't?"

Aiden choked a little, possibly trying and failing to hide a laugh. "I don't know why your mom can't cook, but your grandmother taught me. You'll like her. She's also a bit stubborn. And I don't see how it can be boring. We hung out in a car and had fun, didn't we?"

If she wasn't holding a mug, Chelsea might have applauded him. In her opinion, he'd handled the whole exchange wonderfully. Maybe she'd underestimated him.

• • •

AIDEN

He had no idea what he was doing. Something about having a daughter made him think back to how his parents raised him, but he felt like he was sloshing around in a storm-tossed sea, guessing what might be the right way to handle things without a hope of making the right choices.

The one thing he knew for sure was that he didn't want to fail her. He had years to make up for and not a lot of time to do it. It would help if he felt more connected to the kid, but he just didn't, which made him feel worse.

He'd barely slept the night before, Googling articles about adopting kids—since he got his partially grown, and he hoped to read about how to make himself feel attached. Most of the things he read talked about how they felt something right away, some magical familial bond that he lacked.

But she didn't *feel* like his. It felt like he was spending time with someone else's child. He guessed most parents wouldn't have his particular problem, but most parents had some warning, time to adjust to the idea of becoming a parent. He'd literally had the idea thrust upon him in his office without a moment of warning.

Finally, at somewhere around three in the morning, he'd found an article that suggested what he was going through might not be entirely unique to him. Supposedly, he could just fake it until he felt the fatherly vibes or whatever. So he tried to do just that. He made pancakes. He laid down the law.

Which resulted in a staring contest with his stubborn child. "Seriously, the outdoors won't bite. You can come off the porch."

She crossed her arms, not amused by him in the slightest. "I can do lots of things. The question is, do I *want* to do them? Right now, I want to stand here. If there are interesting rocks out here, find me one."

He glanced around. Seeing a stone on the ground which looked promising, he picked it up and offered it to the bundle of red hair and joy. "Here, this one looks cool."

"That isn't even a rock. That's a piece of broken concrete or something."

He sighed. *Fake it*, he reminded himself. "Okay, you might be right. But can we ask ourselves why there might be a fragment of concrete next to a log cabin?"

"Building the cabin. Next question?" She smirked at him, the little brat.

"You're not making this easy on me," he began.

"Father's Day at school hasn't been easy for me."

Dammit, the kid had a point. He breathed out deeply, wondering where in the hell his assistant was. Didn't he bring her along specifically to make this whole transition easier?

Then again, that did seem a heavy weight to lie on her already overburdened shoulders. Her lovely shoulders.

It would help if he could stop thinking about kissing his assistant. He scrubbed a hand across his face, wishing the answers would somehow magically appear for him.

"Hey, what's that?" his daughter asked. She was practically running off the porch, headed right into the trees where he'd wanted her. Outside, to enjoy the beautiful day and…

Once he saw her destination, he yelped in panic. "Don't touch it! It might have rabies or fleas or…"

It was too late. She was touching it. In fact, she'd scooped it up and was hugging it to her chest. "I always wanted a pet!" Waverley enthused.

"I'm not even sure what that thing is. Probably you shouldn't touch it. Put it back in its natural environment. Yeah, I'm sure that is what you should do. You're disturbing the ecosystem." He took a step back when she got closer to him with the thing.

"It's a cat, Dad, not a part of the natural ecosystem. Geez." She rushed past him, leaving him standing in shock.

It wasn't the cat-like creature that froze him in his tracks. No, she was probably right, although she might get scratched by the beast and need medical care.

It was that one word. She'd called him Dad. For some reason, it shook him to his core and made him finally feel something.

Something good. Something warm. Something warm and fuzzy, even.

Shaking off his shock, he rushed toward the house. She'd carried the bag of fleas and disease with claws into the cabin, and he needed to make sure she was safe. He didn't want that thing to hurt his Waverley.

His. He had a daughter. And she'd called him Dad.

Chapter Nine

Chelsea

"It's a cat," Chelsea said, staring down at the creature in question. Apparently a very docile one, based on the way that Waverley hugged it. The creature didn't seem to mind it, butting its big head against the little girl's chin.

"Yes, I'm going to name him Hematite. Like the black rock? Because he's my little gemstone, aren't you, baby?" The cat responded with a louder purr that seemed to rattle the child's jaw.

"He's kind of dirty," Chelsea said. "And if you're going to keep him, we need some supplies. One sec."

Without hesitation, she pulled her phone out of her back pocket and messaged the head of the security team. She wasn't sure if Chris Ralph was in the team who traveled with them—since the team had remained surprisingly unobtrusive, no doubt out of concern for their young charge—or still back at the office, but she knew he'd be able to coordinate regardless of his position.

He answered her fast, so she asked if he could send a member of the on-site team out for some basic cat supplies—litter pan, cat litter, cat food, maybe a toy or two, and…flea medicine, just in case. He responded back with *no problem*, adding that he felt the team there was likely not doing much anyway. *They said they're mostly playing cards*, he said with a smiley emoticon.

Aiden entered the room from the porch door, and she glanced up and saw that he looked shell-shocked. "You okay, boss man?" she asked.

He shook his head, so she left the child with the cat for a moment to get closer to Aiden. "What happened?" she whispered.

"She called me Dad," he answered. "Chels, she called me Dad."

Impulsively, she reached out to squeeze his hand. "That's good. I mean, since you are."

He blinked fast, and she wondered if he was holding back tears. Something about seeing the powerful man shaken like that melted some part of her she didn't want to look at too closely.

"Thanks," he said simply.

"No problem. Now, to give your daughter's new cat a bath…"

His expression turned steely fast. "She's not keeping it."

She ignored him, figuring she was about to get clawed to pieces. Retrieving the animal from Waverley, she held it while she ran a sinkful of warm water. She figured dish soap would work okay to clean it up, since they used it on animals that were caught in oil spills. Expecting the worst, she slowly lowered Hematite into the makeshift bath.

Much to her surprise, the cat didn't seem to mind the water. "You're a weird cat," she told him as she bathed him as quickly as possible. She didn't want to press her luck—he could decide against tolerating the bath any moment, and his claws looked daunting.

He had a few hitchhiking seed pods stuck in his tail, so she worked those free before rinsing him carefully. She read somewhere that soap was bad for an animal's hide, so she tried to be diligent about getting it all, while the cat still continued to purr.

"I'll be right back," Waverley said, running to another room.

"I sincerely think that thing is a hazard and we should return it to the wild." Chelsea ignored him, much as Waverley had from what she'd seen. Just to annoy him, she leaned down to kiss the cat's head.

Aiden practically twitched. She toweled off the animal in question, still surprised at how easy it had been to bathe the feline. Almost as if it knew they'd rescued it, the cat tolerated the bath and now being dried without notable complaint.

"It is a cat, not a thing. And I have no idea where you think we are, but cats aren't wildlife in the Grand Canyon. At least not this variety. This is just a housecat." Chelsea looked at the battered black bundle in her arms. It was a male, and his ears proved he'd probably seen some interesting things while he'd ventured outside. A regular scarred knight of a cat, the animal had the face of a hardcore old man and one fang that was too big for his mouth. It caused his mouth to gape open just enough for drool to dribble out when he purred.

Which he'd practically done nonstop since Waverley rescued him from outside. Since he had no collar, they couldn't tell whether he'd been abandoned a long time or was just lost, but he needed a bath either way. Chelsea planned to see if he had a microchip by visiting whatever local vet she could find online in the morning, but for the night…

Waverley wasn't willing to let him go. The security team returned with the requested kitty litter, a pan, and other things they might need. The little girl was over the moon. She took the bag and went to set up the creature in her room while Chelsea finished up the bath.

So it looked like they had a handsome four-legged roommate. Chelsea loved him already. Her dad never let her have a pet growing up, other than rocks, and her current apartment didn't allow animals. She'd always wanted one, though, and this fellow had her heart squarely in his pretty black paws.

"What if it has fleas? Disease?" Aiden asked.

She glanced at him over her shoulder. Gone was the arrogant businessman she worked with daily. The vibrant bossiness was swept away in a tide of worried frustration. He was less intimidating like this, making it hard to remember that a suave and sharp billionaire lurked behind the worried eyes he currently focused on the feline.

She remembered his questions and fought to find a suitable response which might comfort him about their furry companion. "I would've noticed if he had fleas when I bathed him. He doesn't. As to disease, he looks pretty healthy to me."

"Then why are his ears dinged up?" Aiden pointed, as if she hadn't noticed. "Healthy cats have full ears. He doesn't."

"Battle scars," she answered. "Look, do you want me to take this cat to the vet or to the local APL tonight? Because it will break your daughter's heart, but I'm willing to do whatever you need me to do. You pay my checks, not her."

Chelsea would also hate to see the cat go, but probably it would be for the best. The longer they spent with him, the more attached she got. Besides, leaving for a while would be good for her sanity. Being this close to him wasn't doing good things for her little crush. Seeing him acting like a regular guy made him far too accessible. Too normal.

Too boink-able, if she were entirely honest with herself. Some time away might be just the ticket for reminding herself exactly who he was and why her fascination with him was ridiculous.

His frown said more than anything else. "What harm can it do in one night?"

As if realizing his only true opponent was caving to his presence, the cat wiggled free of Chelsea's grip to twine himself around Aiden's legs, his purr so loud it practically vibrated the man's jeans.

"None that I know of. But if you're not comfortable..."

"Hematite," called Waverley from the other room. "Oh, there you guys are. Hey, Hemy, are you ready for your dinner? I got him a can of tuna, if that's okay, Chelsea. I found it in the cabinet. I Googled what cats like, and the answer seems to be meat."

"He'd like that, Waverley." Chelsea watched the child scoop up the large cat and rush from the room, then slanted another glance at Aiden. "You know, if she gets attached to him and he doesn't have a home, the next thing she's going to ask is if she can keep him."

The expression on the man's face changed so abruptly, it was like the insecurities and worries were never there to begin with. He transformed seamlessly into her boss, the guy she saw every day in the office, in the space between one heartbeat and the next. "Well, that would become Margo's problem, wouldn't it? I think maybe she does need a pet..."

The slow, Grinch-like smile shouldn't have done it for Chelsea, but it did. "I'm pretty sure she won't go for that."

Before she could move away, he'd spun in her direction and backed her into the sink behind her with nothing more than his presence. "I have a way of convincing people to do what I want them to do, if you'll recall." The power and masculine charisma seemed to flow off him in waves, battering her resolve and making her want to melt into a puddle.

"Glerk," she responded.

His smile grew. Slowly, his fingertip traced down from her temple to her cheek. "I didn't quite catch that."

Her mind raced. How quick would he fire her if she leaned forward and took just a little nibble of that delectable bottom lip of his? The one that spoke of sin and hours of pleasure so great it made a girl's toes curl just thinking about it…

She wasn't in a position to play sexy games with a man like Aiden Kelley. She'd lose, every single time. He wasn't for the likes of her. "Nothing, sir. Just thinking that you did have a talent for business and shouldn't be underestimated. I'm sure Margo will agree to keeping the animal, if you asked."

She'd backed down, and she knew it. The thing was, based on the look on his face, he knew it, too.

It must've been her overactive imagination, because she thought he looked a bit disappointed. Which was crazy, but…

"Chicken," he said before walking away from her.

It took her long moments to translate what he could've meant by that single word. By the time she did, he was long gone, but her fury boiled over anyway.

"Oh, you think I'm a chicken, Aiden? You've messed with the wrong girl if you think I'll back down next time. I dare you to get all sexy like that with me again. I just dare you."

Lucky for her, he wasn't around to hear her. Wouldn't he just laugh at her then?

…

CHELSEA

Chelsea was surprised to see him still awake. She'd thought he went to bed a while ago.

Earlier, they'd played some board games, cared for the cat, eaten a wonderful dinner they'd made together and, afterward, the kiddo had closed herself into her room with Hemy. When Chelsea popped her head in to check on her more than an hour ago, she'd been snoring gently with the bedraggled cat guarding her from the foot of the bed. She'd stared at the two of them for a few moments, long enough for the cat to slow blink a few times before dozing back to sleep, and found peace in how content they both looked.

But a storm had rolled in since then. The thunder and lightning never had a calming effect on Chelsea, so she'd hoped to make a cup of tea and settle down in front of the television, maybe stream some episodes of *Friends* or something until she felt drowsy enough to sleep.

Instead, she stared at the back of Aiden's head as he sprawled on the couch she'd hoped for, his feet carelessly propped up on the coffee table in front of him. Some sports show was on, a ticker at the bottom of the screen giving multiple scores, all of it a jumble of things she didn't really care about.

She decided to tiptoe back out. He'd never know she'd even been there. She turned and snuck partway down the hall before his voice stopped her. "You need something?"

How had he even known she was there? Also, why was she sneaking away? He'd called her chicken, and she wasn't exactly disproving the accusation by slinking back to bed like he'd spooked her away. But before she could come up with any kind of logical response, the lights blinked once and then went out entirely.

The hallway was creepily dark, and she just shoved back a squeak.

"Hey, you okay? Looks like the storm knocked out the power." His voice came from right behind her, just above her right ear, and she jumped in response. "Calm down. It is okay. Just me. You're not scared of the dark, are you, Chels?"

His hands rubbed up and down her arms in a comforting way, and some weak and girlish part of her wanted to melt into his arms. But he was her boss, and that wasn't appropriate, so she steeled her spine and nudged her own chin up. His eyes were a glitter in the darkness. "I'm fine. You just startled me is all."

A flash of lightning had her jolting again and illuminated his sexy face. If he'd looked even a little amused, she thought she might have been able to stomp off to her room in a huff, annoyed with them both. Instead, he looked genuinely concerned, and it put her off balance. It wasn't often Aiden Kelley looked gentle.

"I need to go check on Waverley, but if you can't sleep, go into the living room. Light a candle or two. I'll be back in a minute." He released her arms and moved past her in the general direction of his daughter's room.

She didn't move. For one, she knew better than to hang out alone with him in the dark. She should go to her own room, close the door, and pinch her eyes closed. The storm would likely abate soon, and she was grown up enough to wait it out. Wouldn't be her first storm on her own, after all.

Another bolt of lightning and crash of thunder, sounding way too close, shattered her attempt at calming herself and made her stare into the night, trying to see. Storms were so much worse when they hit at night, and she couldn't see what was coming next. Trees whipped back and forth against the only somewhat less black sky. Lightning arced from cloud to cloud in spider-like fingers, chilling her to the bone. Were there tornados in this area? Floods? What if the wind knocked one of those trees into the house?

Fear froze her in place, and she couldn't even go into the living room as he'd suggested. She hated storms, illogical as the fear might be. They scared the bejesus out of her.

"Gorgeous, isn't it?" His voice again appeared out of nowhere and startled her. "You're really jumpy. You don't like storms?"

She couldn't answer him, couldn't admit to the stupid fear,

even as her hands were ice and her breath raced out too fast.

"C'mon. I'll get us a drink, and we can wait it out together. As of now, Waverley and that creature are still asleep, but I want to be around if they wake up." He sounded so calm, she wished some of it would leech into her. But she could only follow him as he led her by one arm to the living room. Not that the room was an improvement. Floor-to-ceiling windows decorated one wall, stretching high into the cathedral ceiling. They gave a stunning view of the horrible storm, and she gripped the back of the couch, sure they'd both be fried by lightning any second.

So this is how it ends…

He lit a candle and then offered her a tumbler of amber liquid. When she didn't reach out to take it, he cupped her hand around the glass and said softly, "Here. Sip it. It should help."

Alcohol sounded like a damn fine idea, so she slung the likely expensive whiskey back in one gulp. Holding the glass out, she ignored his amused smirk as he refilled it. She chugged it as well.

"Take it easy. I was hoping to take the edge off, not get you hammered. Better?" He still sounded calm and gentle, but it grated on her nerves a little. Couldn't he see how bad this storm was?

In a few minutes, maybe the warmth and burn of the booze would return feeling to her numb fingers, but for now, she worked to focus on him instead of the storm churning outside.

She fucking hated storms.

"You going to say anything at all?" he asked.

Yes, actually… "You said you weren't rich as a kid?"

His smile was confused. "Yeah, why? Sorry, I'm not following your train of thought…"

"Did you ever play in the street? Like, where traffic was?

You know, like kickball or whatever, and when cars came, you yelled 'Pause!' and got everyone off the street. When it was clear, you called 'game on?'" Another crash of thunder shook the windows, and she wondered how the kid could sleep through it. She closed her eyes, hoping for strength but only finding more fear. She really just needed to get her mind off it...

"Sure," he said. "We called 'pause' when there were cars until we could play again. Still not following you, though. Do you have a point?"

"You know how I work for you and all that?"

He sighed, and she was close enough to him that his breath ruffled her hair. "Of course."

"Pause," she said. Before she could talk herself out of it, she went up on tiptoes and touched her lips to his.

He didn't move, and she didn't have the bravery to go further with it. They stood there, frozen, his breath whispering across her cheeks and her lips just barely touching his. Between the heat of his body and that coursing through her veins from her impetuous drinking, some warmth managed to seep back into her, and she felt almost safe for a second.

Then another crash from outside and she shuddered, pinching her eyes closed. He must've felt it or taken pity on her, or who knew what his motives were, but his arms closed around her, and his lips slanted across hers. If she'd thought he would bury her fears and distract her, she was right. Nothing mattered outside that moment.

Lazy hunger curled through the kiss, his experience clear in the slow burn of his mouth dragging across hers. His tongue slipped into her mouth, and she twined her arms around his neck to better brace for the sexy torture of his embrace.

She felt the impact of the wall behind her and wasn't sure if the crash she heard was her system going into overdrive or the sound of the storm. He tasted like sin, and she was starved for more. His hands gripped her hips, and she pressed into his body, thrilling at the sexual tension skating across her flesh like fire.

"Chels," he whispered, his mouth tracing a path down her neck.

"Game on," she gasped.

He stilled, backing away to meet her eyes. Another flash illuminated his face. He looked hungry, like he could eat her up in one big bite.

The sight of that look, on *his* face, made her shiver with want. But he wasn't for her, and this was a ridiculous idea. She couldn't play in his league, knew it on a bone-deep level.

Not that she'd been able to resist a taste.

God. At least in two weeks she would tell him good-bye. Then she wouldn't have to look at his face and be reminded of her moment of weakness. Or how wonderful his mouth had felt against hers.

She ducked under his arm and fled as fast as her legs could carry her, only stopping once her bedroom door separated them. Leaning on it, she bit her lip. Everything in her, down to the last cell, wanted to go back out there, climb him like a tree, and let him take her in whatever depraved fashion he might want to try.

Tomorrow, she'd probably be full of regrets. She'd crossed a line, stupidly. He was her boss.

Somehow, she half wished she could quit now, so she could—

What? Go back to her world while he lived in his, high atop the world in a glass tower of money and power? No, she'd be better off as far away from him as possible, since pursuing anything was an act of masochistic idiocy.

"Impossible," she whispered. Not that it stopped the craving burning just below her skin.

Chapter Ten

Aiden

He reminded himself he wasn't the type of man to hit on the help. His parents raised him better than that, and one thing that disgusted him about a lot of his contemporaries was their utter disregard for the feelings of those they considered "beneath" them.

Which just got him to thinking about how much fun they could have if he could get Chelsea beneath him. Or on top of him, her breasts bouncing in time as she rode them both over the cliff of insanity. Whichever, he wasn't picky.

And, again, that was part of the problem. Chelsea knew him. She just found someone else's panties in his office. She worked with him on the days when he was on top of his game, and she worked with him on the days when he was low. She'd been his friend, cheerleader, companion, and coworker for *years*.

Tossing all that out to toss her into a bed? Yeah, he'd worked hard to remind himself it was impossible. That he couldn't. That he shouldn't. Shit, part of him still hoped she'd change her mind and not quit at all.

Yet today, he gazed at the back of her head while she tried to convince the cat to walk on a leash and couldn't stop thinking about just that. Could he just say, "Pause!" and nip her delicate earlobe between his teeth?

No, he couldn't.

But her mouth last night had been liquid fire under his own. Her body fit his hands in a way he'd never guessed another could. And the little noises she made? Hell, he didn't remember where they were or care.

He needed to keep his distance. To remind himself she was off limits. That she was leaving soon. Maybe he would've pursued something before Waverley, but he needed to focus on what was best for his daughter now. To focus on the things that needed done, not the fact he wanted to do his assistant.

The Grand Canyon spread out before them looking… grand and all. He wasn't nearly as interested in the striations of rock as his daughter, but he had to admit it was big. "Is it what you'd hoped?" he asked Waverley.

She turned around from her spot atop a rock and stared at him. Her eyes were wide and her expression awed. "I don't know what I expected. But it is fabulous. Do you know that the Grand Canyon is the only place where you can look back in time like this? Like, thousands of years."

"No, I didn't know that. But it is pretty cool." He didn't think he could see back in time thousands of years. He could see rock, weathered by time and water, carved into a deep hole. Then again, science never was his favorite subject. He did well in math, and he liked inventing…but rocks kind of all looked the same to him.

Waverley jumped down from her rock and claimed Hematite's leash and returned to snapping pictures with her phone of the cat and the canyon. Which left Chelsea's hands empty for all of three seconds before she'd pulled out her own phone and began clicking at it rapidly.

"You're not working, are you?" he asked.

She glared at him a second before mumbling something that sounded distinctly like, "Well, someone has to. The business won't run itself, after all, and here we are, trotting around a canyon when the James deal is still new and we have a ton of..."

"I hate it when you mumble," he reminded her.

Again the glare, but it vanished when he stepped closer to her. With the tips of his fingers, he brushed the hair off her forehead. He didn't even try to hide the pleasure that had to be evident in his gaze as he watched her catch her breath.

"I'm texting a friend," she quickly assured him. She also took a step away from him, looking at her phone as if she could ignore his presence with the tiny handheld device.

"Tell them I said hi," he said, turning back to Waverley. Then again, it didn't matter where he stood or what he was doing. He was aware of Chelsea in a way he wasn't sure he'd ever been aware of someone before. And he was starting to get the feeling that he was going to stay just that aware for a really, really long time.

• • •

CHELSEA

It would help if the man didn't have an ass she could bounce quarters off of. Then again, she doubted that anyone would dare bounce a quarter or any other denomination of coin money off the ass of a billionaire. *He says hi*, she texted to Kimmie.

The only thing better than a picture of his ass print on a desk would be a picture of his actual ass, Kimmie answered. *You're staying in the same house. Surely, you can accidentally catch him in the shower. Something. Come on. Help a pal out.*

She didn't dare confess that she'd practically molested her boss during the storm the night before. If she told Kimmie that, she'd go positively rabid for details. So instead, she just answered, *I'll get right on that.*

She kept expecting to feel some kind of shame for her behavior the night before, but so far, so good. Instead of feeling embarrassed for kissing her boss after shooting whiskey, she instead was filled with *what if* kind of questions.

What if she had waited to call *game on*? What if, instead of going to her room like a—well, he'd said it—chicken, she would've stayed? Would his hands have wandered? What if she'd let the moment just spin out...?

No, it was stupid and a practice in futility to even consider possibilities that were, realistically, impossible. If the kiss had affected him—which it hadn't, clearly—he would've acted differently the morning after. And so far, *nada. Nothing. Zilch.*

They were back to normal Aiden and Chelsea interaction, even to the point that he frustrated her so much that she talked to herself.

Then again, she wasn't his type. That scrap of lace she'd found in his office? That was the kind of woman in Aiden's league. She didn't even own a thong. All of her underwear came in a three or more package. A lot of it had polka dots. She was an executive assistant, not an actress, and surely not a tall, gorgeous model.

And the bra? *Ha.*

She couldn't fill one cup of that magenta bra with both of her breasts. Maybe. He liked women who were sexy and stimulating and made him feel powerful. He was a billionaire. A playboy. He had more sex than...

Well, most anyone, she guessed.

Sure, he'd kissed her back. But she couldn't help wondering if it was a pity kiss. He wasn't a jerk, and he'd known she was upset. Probably he kissed her back to save her the embarrassment of him *not* kissing her back.

After all, she'd practically climbed him like he was a jungle gym.

She needed to stop thinking about it.

"Hey, I found this night tour on my phone," she said to Waverley and Aiden. She turned the screen so they could see it, and she pointed at the description. "If you can stay up late enough, Waverley, it is a total dark tour. Not tonight, but tomorrow is the next available one. We meet at sunset, and we can learn about nocturnal animals indigenous to this region, not to mention see the night sky. You interested?"

"Yes! Sounds great. Can we still do the geology museum tomorrow during the day?" Giving up on trying to get Hematite to walk on the leash, the child now carried the cat. He drooled happily on her shoulder.

"You got it, kiddo," said Aiden, touching the child's head gently.

See, he touched her, too. He was just a touchy kind of guy. Him stroking his hand on Chelsea's face was nothing more than his normal kind of behavior. Anything she thought she felt from him was likely projection. She understood enough psychology to know better than to read into his casual touches.

Even if they curled her toes in her shoes.

"For now, we should probably go grab some lunch. You hungry?" Chelsea forced a smile to her lips, hoping it looked comfortable and easy rather than showing the strain she felt.

"I could eat," Aiden said.

She watched as he strode back toward the SUV, enjoying his ass as he went. Texting Kimmie back, she admitted, *The man does have a very, very nice ass. I get why you're so interested in it.*

Kimmie answered fast. *I knew it photographed well, but no one has seen the actual ass. Not real people anyway. Take one for the team, Chelsea. Get that ass.*

Snickering, she pocketed her phone. If only life were that simple. A man like him literally could not be interested in a normal kind of girl like her. She knew it logically.

Now to figure out why she was so damn disappointed by the fact.

Chapter Eleven

Aiden

Since the kiddo had been in bed for over an hour, the first sneaking sound technically could've been her. Up for a late night snack or otherwise moving around…

However, the little tingle at the back of his neck said Chelsea was near, but he decided to wait her out. He heard things rustling around in the kitchen, but he simply reclined on the couch and tried to focus on the movie or the game on his phone.

Literally anything but her presence a mere room away.

It wasn't working, and his mind kept giving him possible ways to drive the conversation back to the whole *game on* discussion. He could go out to the kitchen, stand behind the open refrigerator door, then, when she closed it, whisper, "Pause," before leaning in to sample her lips again. "Midnight snack," he could add, with a grin.

Then she'd fall into his arms, and they'd end up tangled on the floor of the kitchen.

Nope, he told his hormones. *Too creepy*.

He was concentrating so hard on not concentrating on her that he didn't notice she'd left the kitchen until she flopped onto the couch next to him. "What are you watching?" she asked.

It took him a few seconds of staring at the screen before he realized he had no clue what the name of the movie was or what happened so far in it. "Just a movie," he answered lamely.

"Huh," she answered. When she took a bite of the cheesecake they'd picked up at a little local store, he watched. The way she licked her lips and then curled them into a slow, sexy smile should come with a warning label.

"So you went to summer camp as a kid," he said, since she'd told him as much on the drive. "What other games did you guys play?"

"Camp games?" she asked. Twirling her fork, she seemed to think back. "I don't know. I already taught you Name that Tune and The License Plate Game."

"That was it?" he asked. "Guess I didn't miss much. I thought maybe you'd have something in mind we could play. Since Waverley is in bed, after all, and neither of us is sleepy."

Her brown eyes focused on him, and she smirked. "There were other games. Telephone is a game where one person whispers something, and then everyone else tries to repeat it, and at the end, you have some hilarious garbled mess that was nothing like the original message. It requires more people, though, for it to work. Um, we played Twenty Questions. In that game, one person has a thing in mind, and everyone gets to ask them questions to try to guess what it is. Kind of like Animal, Mineral, Vegetable, now that I think of it. And… well…" Her blush said whatever came to mind must've been much more interesting, but she didn't complete her thought.

"Now you've got to tell me." He leaned back farther in his

seat, trying to look relaxed, when he actually wanted to lean closer to her. For some reason, although other women didn't make him nervous in the slightest, Chelsea had the unique ability to make him feel off center.

Off balance.

Off his game.

He had a sneaking suspicion it was because other women didn't matter, not in the long run. And Chelsea?

She mattered.

The lady in question took another bite of her cheesecake before sipping the glass of wine she'd brought in from the kitchen. "There were other, more risqué games. Not for the little kids, but for the older ones. Games that the camp counselors probably wouldn't have been as thrilled with, but we found…amusing."

He gestured at the fire. "We have a fire, and this is kind of like a camp. Educate me."

She shook her head. "It wouldn't be appropriate."

He wanted to say *pause*, but he feared he'd be overstepping in some way. Any other time, he didn't hesitate to negotiate or ease his way into whatever deal he wanted. With her?

He simply waited.

"You're actually curious?" she asked.

He turned off the television and shifted in his seat to face her more fully. "Were they dirty?"

She snickered. "Not really. Well, Seven Minutes in Heaven was dirty. In that game, you went into a cabin with a person and…well, stuff happened."

Clearly a kid's game, because nothing he had in mind for Chelsea would take so little time. "What games were naughty but not dirty?"

"Truth or Dare could get kinda risqué. As could Two Truths and a Lie." She set her plate down and licked her lips. "I'm sure you've heard of both of those, though."

"Yeah, I have. Wanna play one?" The last thing he wanted was for her to go to bed. He hadn't been sleeping well, not the entire trip, and thoughts of her would surely make this night no different.

"I like asparagus. I can play the flute. I was raised by my dad." She rattled the three sentences off so fast, it took him a second to realize what she'd done.

"I was hoping you'd go with Truth or Dare, but I'm going to guess that the lie was the part about the flute?" He reached out and brushed at that lock of hair, the one that always fell over her forehead.

He wasn't sure if it was his response or his touch that caused it, but she blushed prettily. "Correct. Why did you hope I'd pick Truth or Dare?"

The smile crawled slowly to his lips. "Unless we're playing, I don't have to tell the truth."

"Fine, Truth or Dare, Aiden."

She so rarely said his name, preferring for the most part to call him Mr. Kelley unless he'd annoyed her, so he reveled in that for a second before he went with the safe response. "Truth."

"Now who is the chicken?" she asked, laughing. In yoga pants and a tank top, she looked less like his assistant and more like a woman. A very sexy and comfortable woman. The intimacy should've scared him, but it didn't. It was Chelsea.

She was special.

"You don't have a question?" he teased.

"What is your most embarrassing moment?" she responded so quickly that he guessed she had the question ready to begin with.

"Okay, I was maybe fourteen? Anyway, young. And I had a crush on my teacher. Her name was Miss Meadows, and she was the most beautiful woman I'd ever met. On top of that, she could sing. What more can a guy want, right?" Her laugh encouraged him, so he continued. "So I did what any guy would do. For Valentine's Day, I bought her a flower. You know, one of those ones that they deliver in class? They sell them for a buck or whatever to raise money for the class... Anyway, I wrote out the card to the most beautiful woman in the world, as one does."

Chelsea nodded. "Of course. How else would you address it?"

"Right? And I signed it. But I realized she'd get in trouble if she admitted her undying love for me in return, so I erased my name back off the card and figured I'd be, like, a secret admirer."

"Logical," she agreed.

"Exactly. You could tell, even then, that I was a particularly brilliant guy. And so the flower got delivered, right there in front of the whole class. I sat there, front row, waiting to see her response. She blinked in surprise then did something teenage me didn't expect."

"What did she do?"

"She held the card up to the light. Did you know that, if you press hard when you're writing—to try to look grown up by making sure your penmanship is perfect—and then erase what you've written, it is still clearly visible on construction paper just by holding it up to the light?" He pretended to hold an imaginary square and then imitated the expression on her face when she'd looked at him.

"Nope, did not know that."

He shook his head sadly. "Me either. Needless to say, she asked to see me after class. Now, I admit...I thought maybe it would still work out for me. I gave her a flower, it was Valentine's Day...but she just wanted to tell me that, although I was a very nice boy and one of her all-time favorite students, it wasn't going to work out. She said I should consider a girl my own age."

She covered her lips with her hand, hiding her smile. "Did you take her advice?"

He shrugged. "Not your turn for a truth."

"Touché," she responded.

"Truth or dare?" he asked.

Her hand dropped, revealing a mischievous smile. "Dare."

"You're just trying to prove you're not a chicken," he pointed out.

"Is it working?"

"Not really," he said. "But good try. Dare you to wear a finger moustache for a full turn."

"A what?"

"Like this," he said and demonstrated by holding his finger above his upper lip. "As you can see, it is a classic look."

She snickered. "Not where I thought you'd go with this, but fine. Finger moustache. Happy?"

He laughed outright. "You look ridiculous. My staid, ever-cautious Chelsea with a finger moustache. Can I post a picture of this to my social media?"

Her glare was impressive, even with the finger moustache. "My turn. Truth or dare, Aiden?"

"Truth," he said, smiling at her beatifically.

"Now who is the chicken?" But her annoyance faded, and she kept on her finger moustache. "What was your scariest memory?"

"Easy. Active duty, overseas. Next question."

The finger moustache dropped. "I didn't know you were in the military."

"You lost your moustache," he pointed out.

She replaced her finger, and her eyebrows dropped low. "You're just going to leave it at that?"

"I'm after you taking your turn, lass. Truth or dare?" He laid the Irish accent on thick, pleased when her breath caught and her eyes locked on his.

He wasn't wrong. For some reason, it turned her on when he used the accent. He locked that little detail away for use on some later date.

She recovered after a second and cleared her throat before answering. "Dare."

He grinned at her. "Don't be offering that if you're going to back out the moment I give you a dare."

She shrugged and changed her response. "Okay, I'll take a truth, then."

"What made you call *pause*?"

Silence filled the room, weighted in sexual tension. "Curiosity. Your turn."

He waved a finger at her like a metronome. "Not getting out of it that easily. What exactly were you curious about, Chels?"

She lost the finger moustache and reached for her wine. "It is human nature, Aiden. I'm a woman, you're a man…it was curiosity."

"Pause," he whispered.

He couldn't do more than that. It was up to her. It had to be.

"Truth or dare, Aiden?" she answered. She set the glass down slowly, not meeting his gaze.

"Which do you want me to pick?"

"I don't know."

He sighed. "Truth, then."

"Did you do it because you pitied me?" She didn't look anywhere near him, as if she feared his response.

"Do what? Wait, does it matter? I never pity you. You're strong, confident, gorgeous… I don't even put pity in the same room as you." He answered honestly, scooting a bit closer to her.

"No, I meant did you kiss me back because you pitied me?" She sounded annoyed, but she at least looked at him again.

"I kissed you because I've wanted to kiss you for a while, and it was the first time I felt like you wouldn't punish me for that desire." Again, the honesty cost him nothing.

She swallowed hard. "Promise?"

The question was a whisper. A moment of her letting down her guard. He saw it for what it was, and he couldn't resist tracing her lips with his fingertip. "Promise. I kissed you because I wanted to."

"Okay," she answered.

"Can I get a redo?" he asked.

Her frown returned. "You want to revoke that answer already?"

"Nope. Ask me truth or dare, Chels." He practically held his breath, hoping she'd do what he wanted her to.

"Truth or dare?" she asked. The words were so soft, they were hardly more than a whisper of air. But he heard her.

"Dare," he answered with confidence.

"Dare you to kiss me like you mean it?"

"With pleasure," he responded.

• • •

CHELSEA

This time, the seduction wasn't lazy. His mouth on hers set her blood on fire. He pressed into her, forcing her back on the couch and drowning her in his taste. He was her new official favorite smell—like her darkest desires given scent. His hands traced up her ribs, electrifying her nerve endings and scorching her senses. In any of her imaginings of what being in Aiden Kelley's arms would be like, she'd never dreamed up anything as passionate as the actual man.

He stopped just shy of cupping her breasts, though, lifting his head. "If this isn't what you want, you can change your mind."

"I want you," she admitted. The words might damn her, but she couldn't drum up the reserve to care. "I want *you*, Aiden."

"Not here," he said. Without further explanation, he lifted her from the couch and began to carry her. She wrapped her arms around his neck, surprised.

"You're carrying me," she whispered into his neck. Heat flooded her face. She wasn't light, and she hadn't lost that fifteen pounds... Hell, she'd been eating cheesecake.

Not that her weight seemed to be an issue for him, since he strode down the hallway like she wasn't a burden in the least.

"Yes," he answered, pinching her ass with the hand holding it. "I am."

He carried her into his bedroom, careful to close and lock it behind him before leaning on the door. "I wanted the time to explore you without worrying about an interruption," he explained.

"Oh," she whispered. He still hadn't put her down, so she gave his neck an experimental lick, which he rewarded with a small moan. In seconds, he'd taken her lips again, only releasing her enough that her body dragged down his before her feet reached the floor.

She decided that, for this night, he wasn't the Aiden Kelley from the office. He was hers, at least for the time they had together. And she was going to squeeze every last drop of pleasure out of what time they had. Part of her feared that, if he remembered who she was—not a model or actress and actually just a boring assistant—he'd change his mind.

But how could he not remember? She wasn't sexy or suave, not really. Which underwear was she wearing? *Please don't let me be wearing a pair that has a hole in them...*

"You're thinking so loud, I can practically hear it," he

whispered. His fingertips traced across her collarbone before those gorgeous eyes of his met hers. "Stop."

Her breath came out on a jagged exhale. His face showed only desire—for her.

He might normally want women who were miles out of her league, but this night? He wanted her. It would be enough.

It *had* to be enough.

She met his lips again, hoping to drown out her insecurities, but he ended the kiss and instead put space between them. "I want to see you," he explained.

What would he see? She wasn't anything like what he usually had in the bedroom—or the office. "I—"

"Let me see you, Chels," he said. His face looked sincere and adoring, so she couldn't refuse his request.

He slid her top off with a gentle motion, following the fabric up her ribs with kisses. If she thought he might be put off by her bra, his carnal smile nixed that notion. "Truth or dare?" he whispered.

"Dare," she responded.

"Dare you to remove your breasts from the bra but leave it on," he answered, licking his lips.

"You're even bossy in the bedroom, you know that?" she teased, but she obeyed, loving the way he seemed completely fascinated by her movements. His hands came forward, thumbs just barely grazing her nipples and making her gasp.

"You have no idea," he said. He tugged off his own shirt impatiently before pulling her close so their chests rubbed together as his mouth took hers again. The contact sizzled her ability to think, fried all logic. His palms grazed under her yoga pants and underwear, cupping her ass as he lifted her until she wrapped her legs around his waist.

She scraped her nails along the hard muscles of his back, reveling in the hot feel of his smooth skin under her hands. Nipping at his neck, she gasped when he swung into motion.

In seconds, she found herself on the bed. "On your knees," he ordered.

Obediently, she knelt, but she figured it was her turn. "Truth or dare, Aiden?"

"Dare," he responded without the least hesitation.

"Strip," she said. "Nice and slow."

His grin was devilish. "As you wish." He unbuttoned his jeans before gliding his hands upward, across that dent of musculature which seemed to point between his legs. She caught her lip between her teeth, watching in fascination as he spun away from her and inched the pants down, slowly revealing that ass she couldn't seem to resist.

He paused, glancing back at her before he moved his body in one fast wave that removed the pants and revealed his entire back and ass to her.

As he turned back to face her, she stared at his cock, proud and hard as it practically pointed at her.

He was hard. For her.

She reached for him, and he again waved his finger in front of her. "Uh uh. Truth or dare, Chels?"

Frustrated, because she wanted to touch him, she glared at him. "Now he wants to play games?" she grumbled.

"Don't mumble," he reminded her with a smile.

"Dare," she answered.

"Your turn. Strip for me."

She couldn't do sexy, so she didn't bother trying, removing her clothes in a rush. He helped, though, his hands seeming to touch each inch of flesh she revealed seconds before his mouth spread kisses along her spine, her wrists, everything.

He seemed determined to mark each inch of her flesh with his kisses, and she couldn't think of a single complaint to that idea.

"Kneel again," he said.

"It isn't your turn," she replied with a gasp. His lips were at her waist, nibbling at her hip.

He smacked her ass in response. She growled and pulled his hair but decided that obeying him in this case likely would be in her favor. Once she was on her knees, she was surprised to see him kneel on the floor. He urged her forward, so she knelt just at the edge of the bed.

"New dare," he said.

"Still not your turn," she grumbled, but she was lost in his hungry gaze and likely would do whatever he asked.

Apparently, he knew it as he said, "Spread your legs for me."

She did, as much as she could while kneeling at the edge of the bed, and he rewarded her motion by kissing her just there…

"Oh," she whispered, gripping his hair. "Aiden…"

But soon his tongue and lips had her wordless. His palms held her in position, only allowing her some movement as she jerked her hips toward his talented mouth. It was too much.

It was everything.

Her body ignited, fire shooting from the heat between her legs to scorch her every nerve. She spasmed, the orgasm almost catching her by surprise, only his controlling hands keeping her from melting off the bed in a puddle.

But he wasn't done with her. Oh no, he slid her back onto his big, decadent bed and seized her lips with his own. Imprisoned by his weight, she didn't think she could do more than gasp. But then his clever fingers had her arching again, bucking against him as he seemed to play with her body as if he knew it better than she herself did.

Maybe he did.

Her hands were busy as well, cupping him, stroking him as he suckled at her breast. "Aiden," she whispered.

"I know," he answered, reaching toward the nightstand. In seconds, he'd covered his beautiful cock with a condom and then used it to tease at the slit between her legs. "Chels, I need you," he admitted.

She opened for him, welcoming him home as he sank into her body. In desperation, she moved with him, rising to meet him and draw him deeper. She couldn't keep her eyes open, but he locked their mouths in a kiss that swallowed her shout as she came again on a cry of his name.

Chapter Twelve

Chelsea

Morning sunlight on her cheek warmed her face, and she stretched luxuriously, feeling like a cat in a welcoming sunbeam. But then the weight around her waist shifted, hugging her closer, and she froze.

She was in Aiden Kelley's bed.

Her boss.

Shit, shit, shit. Well, she was sure she could find another job. Because he would surely fire her. *Or give me a raise…*

Stop that, she told herself. *Quit being an idiot.*

But her brain refused the request, instead second guessing everything they'd shared. He'd woken her twice in the night, each time thrilling her, because it seemed that he couldn't get enough of her.

Probably because he's a sex addict, her brain unhelpfully suggested. *And you're convenient right now. Location, location, location…*

Not to mention she'd be leaving in two weeks. Probably

things would be different if there wasn't a set expiration date on their connection, but there was no risk for him whatsoever. She'd be out of his hair one way or another in no time flat.

"D'ya know you even complain in your sleep?" His voice was right in her ear, a small growl of a whisper. The scruffy feel of his face buried itself into her shoulder before his hand slid up her stomach and across her ribs to find a breast. Kneading the breast in question in a sensual way that made her squirm against him, he continued, "So I figured every time you woke me up, I'd wake you up. I gotta admit, Chels, I've never had so much fun getting woken up repeatedly in my life."

She opened and closed her mouth, trying to think of a proper response, but then he bit her earlobe, sending a shower of sparks across her skin. The words she couldn't find turned into a small moan.

He rolled on top of her, taking her mouth in a long, slow, and hungry kiss. When he came up for air, she managed to find her words. "I didn't hear you complaining."

As he rubbed against her, he laughed gently in her ear. "Not complaining now, either."

"Dad?" said Waverley before tapping at the door. "You awake?"

They both froze, and Chelsea wasn't sure if she felt guilty or caught, like a kid with her hand in the proverbial candy jar. Aiden placed one fingertip on her lips before answering, "Yes, I'm up, kiddo. I'll be out in a few. Gonna grab a shower. Go ahead and get yourself a bowl of cereal and feed Hemy in the meantime?"

"Okay," said the little girl, her footsteps retreating down the hall.

No sooner was she gone than Chelsea bolted out of the bed. "Oh my god. I'm so sorry. I'll just—"

Where the hell was her bra?

His arms captured her from behind, tugging her back into

his lap. His naked lap. "Calm down. The door is closed. She doesn't know you're in here."

"Yes, well, I know," she answered. "How did I lose my bra?"

She tried to scramble free, but he simply stood and lifted her into his arms. She didn't get more than a squeak out before he kissed her again.

"You need a shower," he advised.

"I need to…" She trailed off as he leaned her against the bathroom door, suckling her breast into his delightful mouth.

"Get a shower," he repeated as he released the nipple.

"Okay."

His slow smile rewarded her for her positive response. In seconds, he had the shower adjusted. She noticed he seemed blissfully unware of his nudity, while she felt exposed somehow. Like she'd revealed too much, even if it only seemed to take a touch from him to blind her to reality.

Even so, she snagged the tube of toothpaste from the sink and used a little on her fingertip to freshen her breath. Although he seemed not to care about that sort of thing, when he wasn't driving her wild with passion, she remembered common niceties.

But he came up behind her while she still had her finger in her mouth. The multiple bulbs surrounding the bathroom mirror illuminated her naked body in front of his, and she compared them. She wasn't model gorgeous, just rather ordinary, while he was spectacular. Even with that knowledge in place, she couldn't help sucking in a deep breath when his hand cupped her breast. There was something sinfully erotic about both feeling his rough palm against her sensitive skin and seeing it in the glass.

He seemed to know that, because he met her eyes in the reflection. "Watch. Watch what I can do to you, my staid and careful Chelsea."

His teeth came down on her earlobe, startling a shocked sound from her throat. The sound elongated into a moan as he laved the spot and then ran wet kisses down her neck. His hands didn't slow, kneading her breasts and tweaking her nipples, and she sagged against him.

He tsked that action, coming around in front of her. His kiss was hungry, rolling their tongues together and making her go on tiptoes for more. But then he sank to his knees in front of her. "Keep watching the mirror, Chels. Brace your hands on the sink top," he ordered.

"Bossy," she said.

"You have no idea," he said, repeating his sentiment from the night before.

Part of her hoped that meant he was going to prove it. The other part just trembled in desire. His fingertips parted her, and his tongue slid inside, and she couldn't think at all.

He seemed to know just how she needed him to nibble and suck, eating away at her decorum until she literally rode his face for more. When he paused and simply stroked her with his fingertips, she opened her mouth to complain, but he interrupted her.

"You're not watching," he said. "Keep your eyes open and watch the mirror or I'll stop."

"This isn't a game," she growled.

"It is, if we do it right. Watch the mirror." His fingertips kept tracing the lightest touches, frustratingly close but not quite what or where she needed. "Tell me what you see?"

"You have got to be kidding me. He wants me to talk, now of all times?" She glared at her own reflection but didn't try to escape his light hold on her legs.

"And don't mumble." She could feel his smile against her leg after he dropped a light kiss there.

The mirror was beginning to fog with the steam from the bath. "I see myself. My face is flushed..." As if to reward her, he took one long lick from the back of her slit to the front, stopping to toy at her entrance. "Oh, when you do that, my breath speeds up. I—"

He captured the bundle of nerves between his teeth, and his tongue flicked across her clit at what felt like hyper speed. She clutched at the sink, bending over it and resting her head on the faucet as she jerked. "Fuck," she panted.

Then she spiraled over the edge, a low moan escaping her lips to echo against the porcelain. Tremors quaked inside her, and she couldn't move. Couldn't anything except experience the waves of electricity spiraling from her center out to her fingertips.

He stood, capturing her waist and lifting her as he turned to plant her ass on the cold stone sink top. Before she could say anything, he was devouring her mouth, his teeth scraping against her lips as he pressed against her.

She returned his embrace, practically melting into his arms before he lifted her again, carrying her into the steaming shower lined with stone. "Had to let it warm up in here," he explained. "Didn't want you to catch a chill. One sec, let me grab a condom."

As he stepped out of the shower, she said, "I have a sudden appreciation for how you choose to pass the time when forced to wait." In seconds, he returned with the protection.

She couldn't get enough of his skin, kissing him and touching him, and he allowed it. When he grabbed his cock in his own hand to roll on the condom, she practically whimpered.

"You think that is hot enough?" he asked her, giving himself one long stroke.

"Hell yeah," she muttered.

"I meant the water." His slow smile rewarded her, though, as he reached for a bar of soap.

She took it from him, using the suds as an excuse to

explore what seemed like miles of delicious male flesh. Once she began to rinse him, she decided to put that cock in her mouth, just to see if she could make him react as much as he affected her. He was hard, and she cupped the base of his cock as she worked to drive him even an iota as wild as he drove her.

He only lasted a second before he'd pulled her to her feet. "Naughty girl. I thought we agreed that I gave the orders around here." But his hands shook, just a little, where he gripped her arms and his cheeks were flushed.

She smirked at him. "If you think that today is going to be the day that I begin to just listen to you without talking back…"

"Face the wall, Chels."

Her laugh echoed in the shower, but she obeyed, planting her hands slightly above her head. "Like this?" she asked, spreading her legs a little.

"It'll do, to start," he agreed. Then he lifted her at the waist and drove himself deep into her center. His moan was nearly as loud as hers, and she hung there, trying to keep her purchase against the slick walls.

"Trust me, baby," he whispered.

As he began to thrust into her body in a slow and mind-glazing way, she was happy to obey. The angle meant he wasn't able to go deep, but he made up for it with speed. She was close.

So close.

But he stopped again, and she practically growled at him in frustration. "Don't stop," she ordered.

"You aren't the boss," he reminded her. He pulled her up so that her back lined up with his chest, his hands busily swapping between her breasts and the overly sensitized flesh between her legs. The water made his hands slide, and the heat had her rolling her head back to rest on his shoulder.

He took advantage of the position to taste her. "You're so damn sweet. Can't get enough of it."

His words made her smile while his touch made her sigh. Without warning her, he turned her again, seating her on the stone bench in the shower. "What now?" she whispered.

"I didn't want to slip," he said. "And so I could do this."

He tugged one of her legs over his arm and again slid inside her. She moaned as he managed to go deeper, hitting a spot which left her wriggling against him. "Shh," he whispered. "Slowly."

The pace he set was slow and steady, a teasing motion which only stoked the flames inside her, delaying the release that was so close. She slid one hand between them, hoping to ease the burning ache inside her, but he captured the wrist and held it above her head. "Not yet," he explained. "Trust me."

She wanted to protest—to claim she did trust him—but her words came out a keening cry as he suddenly changed the angle and sped up his pace. She used the leg he was holding for leverage, lifting her hips to meet him. She couldn't think. Couldn't breathe.

He was the scent around her, heightened by the water. He was the feel of flesh on flesh. He was her everything. When she tumbled over the edge, he was there to catch her. His arms holding her close as she trembled, his lips soothing her flesh, his heart thudding against her own.

"Good morning," he whispered after a long while of holding her.

"Very good," she answered.

• • •

AIDEN

He couldn't remember ever being in a better mood. A glance

over his shoulder showed Waverley bent over a table model of the canyon. Chelsea was with her, pointing at something, and as if she felt his eyes on her, she looked up and met his gaze.

The smile withered off her face and was replaced by a hunger that matched his own. She blinked twice fast, quickly recovering and going back to her conversation with Waverley, but the day had been full of little moments like that.

As he returned to looking out at the Grand Canyon, he didn't really see the view out the floor-to-ceiling windows. Instead, he wondered what a future with Chelsea in his life could be like. Clearly, she'd already bonded with his daughter, so he didn't foresee any issues on that front. They'd figure it out between the three of them—find a way to fit into the roles none of them expected but they all seemed to be made for anyway.

He and Chelsea already had a working relationship, so fitting her into that part of his life would be pretty simple, too. Sure, there'd be talk around the office for a while, but he knew of other people who'd become involved with coworkers. Some didn't end well, but others…

Well, they did end well, and he knew it. He could easily imagine what previously had been heated debates in his office devolving into him kissing her until they both burned the edge off their frustration, then them going back to work smiling. They'd been together in that way for years, so finding a way to blend the new pleasurable side of their relationship into their preexisting work one shouldn't prove complicated whatsoever in the long run.

But why was he considering the long run? He'd slept with a lot of women over the years and never before tried to think of ways to make the connection last. What made Chelsea different?

For starters, he figured it was because she wasn't just a

lover. She'd been his friend, the person by his side, more than any other over the years. She was the only person willing to put up with his bullshit and still stand up to him, even though he'd never admit he liked those traits. He couldn't imagine a world without her in it or himself without her by his side.

Which was an overly romanticized notion and one he should discard quickly before it took root. He did lots of things without her by his side and probably would do a lot more in the future. He shouldn't put a ton of weight on something that, as of right then, was nothing more than a one-night stand.

But therein lay the root of his problem. He wanted more than one night with her. Not only had he not nearly quelled the craving he seemed to have for her flesh, but he wanted mornings waking her with a kiss. He wanted evenings spent with her grumbling and him teasing her out of her grouchiness. He wanted walks with her when he was stressed and nights of her body curved against his in the darkness.

For some odd reason, the whole consideration brought to mind his parents. They'd never been the type to discuss divorce, even when they had rough patches over the years. Instead, they seemed to come out of every challenge even closer than when they started. They weren't overly affectionate in public, but every so often…

When they thought he wasn't paying attention, mostly, he caught them holding hands. Or when something went wrong, he'd seen that his father's first reaction was to reach for his mother.

That was, really, what he craved for the long term. Maybe he'd never put it to words before, but part of the reason none of his other relationships—if he could call them that—worked out was that they weren't with someone he could see reaching for when he was upset.

Chelsea was already that person for him. And now, she

was his lover, too.

Her hand grazed his side, and he glanced down to meet her warm brown eyes. How would they look when time carved wrinkles into the corners? He tried to imagine it—to imagine forever with her—and found he couldn't.

He might not be able to picture her old, but he could see her smile being something he looked forward to every day. Hell, he'd already been doing just that for years.

"We're about to head to the gift shop to buy some magnets. Care to join?" she asked.

"Yeah," he answered. "I do."

Chapter Thirteen

Chelsea

Waverley peppered the guide with questions and seemed glued to her side, right from the outset of the nocturnal tour. At first, Chelsea lingered toward the back in hopes she wouldn't overstep. *After all*, she reminded herself, *you're here to help him bond with his daughter.*

But it quickly became apparent that Waverley didn't need either of them to enjoy the tour. She stuck by the guide's side, and the woman even held her hand as she asked everyone to turn off their flashlights to better enjoy the light of the stars and the sounds of the creatures around them.

The darkness around them was absolute. Following near to the person in front of her, Chelsea practically bumped into them when they came to a stop. The tour guide's voice carried easily to her ears, even from her position near the back of the group. "If you listen closely, we might be able to hear some owls…"

The guide went on to describe a few of the different kinds

of owls indigenous to the region, but Chelsea tuned her out. She could practically feel Aiden's presence somewhere behind her—a palpable heat that didn't compare to the intensity of the lasting warmth from the day. If she listened very closely, she could even hear his breath.

After a full day of things being normal between them, she craved his touch. Longed to find out if the magic from the night still lingered or if it'd been some kind of weird fluke.

A silly part of her thought they were breathing in tune, synchronized at some cellular level, but likely she actually listened to the sound of the breeze or the other people. At that moment, she realized the group had moved on, the droning of the guide farther in the distance than moments before, but she wasn't alone.

He'd stayed behind with her. "I really do appreciate all you've done for me and Waverley. And I know…I've heard it before. I'm a control freak and an asshole, so I'm lucky you put up with me."

Although he tried to wash the words with a playful tone, Chelsea heard something in his voice that she'd never noticed before. Was it always there, and had she just never paid attention? What she heard was loneliness. Which was silly, really, because a man like him wasn't lonely. He was powerful, handsome, rich…hell, he could buy all the companionship he might want.

But that might be the root of it. Maybe he was like her, looking for a real connection. Looking for someone who saw beyond the curtain to the person inside? "I haven't called you an asshole for ages. I deserve a raise," she joked. Because saying any of the things she was thinking would be idiotic.

Crazy.

Yet she moved closer to the sound of his voice, as if drawn to him. His soft chuckle wrapped her in decadence, and she shivered. "Yeah, you can't call me an asshole, even if I deserve it."

Smiling, she felt the need to remind him, "Nope. I *shouldn't*. Not that it ever stopped me. But you don't pay me for calling you names… I throw that service in for free."

His laugh again, but this time closer. She couldn't help but remember their kiss. When he'd tilted her head back and taken her lips, she'd felt alive for the first time in such a long time. As if none of the rest mattered, just the magic of his skin rubbing against her own.

And then she didn't have to remember because his hand tilted her head and his mouth was on hers. The kiss was slow, lingering for long moments at teasing before it suddenly changed. He went from teasing to plundering in the space between one heartbeat and the next.

Her pulse hammered, as if her heart was trying to beat its way free of the cage of her ribs. His hands traced across her hips and scraped her shirt upward until his hands palmed her breasts over her bra. She arched into the touch, craving more.

He delivered, dragging open-mouthed kisses down her throat as his hand found her breast and then tugged at her nipple. Somehow, one of his legs was between hers, and she bucked against it, riding the denim in a need to get closer. To get more.

His teeth scraped her neck, and she moaned. "Aiden," she whispered.

And his mouth returned to hers, the kiss drowning out the night and anything past the flavor of him. The feel of him.

Her need for him.

She cupped him over his pants, and his head dropped to her shoulder. Something about the powerful man being so vulnerable to her touch just made her hotter. She nipped his chin, and he again kissed her, grabbing her ass to pull her closer.

"I need you," he whispered.

"Yes," she whispered.

"Tonight?" he asked.

She couldn't deny him. She tried to calm her breathing, to remind herself they were in the forest and it wasn't the time or place, but she didn't care.

She wanted him.

"Waverley?" a female voice called. "Waverley, where did you go?"

The sound was like ice being poured down her spine. "Waverley?" she whispered.

Aiden had stilled, his head turned toward the voice. In seconds, he was gone, and her arms felt cold and empty. A sense of foreboding came over her, the same kind she got when the music changed on a scary movie.

Surely, the kid was just a few feet away from the group in the darkness. She couldn't have gone far, not really. But as flashlights lit up the night, Chelsea couldn't see the red hair of the child anywhere in the group.

But she could see Aiden's face. And the look of accusation on his chiseled features carved a hole in her chest.

• • •

AIDEN

He was a fool. He'd only just found his daughter, not knowing she was out there for years without him, and he'd lost her. Margo would never forgive him if something happened to the kid—

Hell, he wouldn't forgive himself.

They were by the Grand Canyon, for Christ's sake. She could've fallen off a cliff. She could be hurt somewhere, bleeding. *Dead.*

The thought froze him in his tracks. What if he'd been fooling around with his assistant against a tree and lost her forever?

No, far more likely she'd been kidnapped. No one *seemed* to have recognized him, but someone might have. It only took one person, desperate enough in need of money, to grab a child and run off with her. They could ransom her. He'd seen stories…

Shit. This was all his fault. He didn't know how to be a father, and he'd failed her.

"Waverley!" he called out again, and he couldn't hide the panic and desperation in his voice.

Please answer me. Please, please, I'll do anything…

"Dad?" came back an answering voice. It was soft, as if she worried she was in trouble or was scared, and it came from somewhere above him rather than on ground level or—worse—from someplace down a cliff side.

He looked up. On a branch that didn't look safe and likely wasn't stable enough for it to support her weight, Waverley perched. She was about five yards from where he stood, illuminated by his flashlight. The little girl let go of the branch with one hand, covering her eyes. "Hey, get the light out of my eyes!"

He quickly re-aimed the flashlight, directing it at the tree next to her, afraid she'd lose her precarious balance and fall because he blinded her with light. At a dead run, he reached her pretty quickly but still wasn't sure how to help her. "Can you get down?" he asked. His tone was sharp, and the kid looked a little nervously at him.

He tried to calm his heartbeat, his fears, so he didn't scare her more, but he just couldn't quite staunch the panic in his chest.

"Well, yeah, if you quit blinding me. I was trying to see if I could get close to the owl."

Her explanation made him feel worse. If he'd been paying attention to her like he should've, she wouldn't have had time to climb a tree.

In the dark.

In the Grand Canyon.

"Okay, well, come on down. Nice and slow." Twice, her foot slipped. Each time, he thought for sure she'd fall, breaking a leg or her neck, but she quickly adjusted herself and managed to get down the tree close enough to the ground for him to scoop her into his arms.

Holding her close, he hugged her until she protested. "Geez, Dad. Don't freak out. I'm fine."

She'd called him Dad again, but he didn't feel he deserved that name. He set her on her feet but couldn't forgive himself for her being endangered in the first place. He'd known better.

He'd been distracted by his dick. He could try to pretty it up however he wanted, by telling himself Chelsea was different and that his feelings for her were more than common lust, but at the end of the day…he'd endangered his child because he'd been thinking about sex.

Chelsea burst into the small clearing between the trees and bent at the waist, panting. "Oh, he found you! Thank God."

"This is all your fault," he snapped before he thought better of it. "You were the one who suggested we go wandering around in the dark in the Grand Canyon. This was all your brilliant idea. If you hadn't distracted me, she never would've been lost to begin with."

Even as he said it, he blamed himself for taking out his fears and panic on her, but once he said it, he couldn't take the words back. Besides, maybe it was for the best. Better to drive Chelsea away now, before he ruined it all and more feelings were involved. He needed to focus on Waverley, not this thing with his assistant.

"I wasn't lost. Like I said, I wanted to see the owl—" Waverley began.

He shook his head. "You're right. That was an overreaction. But I think we've had enough of the Grand Canyon. We're going back to the cabin and flying home in the morning. I'll set up the transportation. When we get back, to bed with both of you. We'll pack and fly out in the morning." Even he could hear how somber his tone had become.

But he already loved Waverley. More than he'd assumed possible, considering he hadn't known about her for long. Not knowing where she was for a few minutes—it terrified him. What would it be like when she went home to her mother? It wasn't like they had an agreement or even that he had legal rights to Waverley at all.

He wanted to be with her all the time.

And he had the right to none of her time, really. He had to think of a way to become part of her life. A solid part. He didn't want to have gotten to know her just to lose her again. There had to be some way to ensure it...

Chapter Fourteen

Chelsea

He'd had the security team seat Chelsea in a separate room on the plane, claiming she could get more rest in the small bedroom. The reason he gave was that they had a lot of work to do once they returned to the office, but he sent her that notification via text, and she hadn't seen him. A member of the security team had driven her to the airport, and although she could hear that Aiden and Waverley had boarded, she hadn't seen either of them.

As a matter of fact, he hadn't said a word to her since the night before in the woods.

He was still mad, and she couldn't even blame him. She'd known the folly of sleeping with her boss before she'd done it, yet it hadn't stopped her. She knew why he invited her on this trip—and it wasn't for sex. He wasn't even wrong—it *was* her fault the little girl had gotten lost. She'd been so busy wanting him to kiss her, to touch her and prove that the moments they'd shared in the night hadn't been a fluke, that she disregarded all responsibilities and...as he'd claimed... distracted him.

It was likely for the best anyway. It wasn't like they were going to begin some long term, meaningful relationship just because they'd had sex in a cabin. What happened on vacation stayed on vacation, right?

And she couldn't even text Kimmie about it. She trusted her friend—she did—but in this case? One slipped word from her could cause a media scandal which would cost Chelsea her job. Not to mention it could expose Waverley... No. She couldn't take that risk, and she wouldn't put Kimmie in that sort of position, anyway.

So it was just her and her circular thoughts, trapped on a plane for a few hours.

Chelsea did what she always did in times of stress or strife. She opened her laptop, pulled up the company email and messaging services, and got to work. There was plenty she could accomplish on the flight home and lots that she'd neglected when she had been distracted by Aiden.

Now, if she could just see past the tears that kept blurring her eyes, she'd be good to go.

The next day at the office wasn't any better. He called her into his office, and instead of even trying to talk about what happened, he simply began rattling off emails for her to send so fast that she had to type quickly to keep up. There was no time for gazing at his face and remembering how it had twisted in passion or how he'd seemed more vulnerable and real over their trip than she'd ever seen him before.

Just work.

They worked right through lunch, so there was no opening for her to ask how Waverley was doing. No chance to see if he'd talked to Margo or ask anything personal whatsoever. She set up his video conference and closed the door to give him privacy, not even able to blink back tears outside his office because she feared someone would see her crumbling and guess at some of what had transpired.

All in all, it worked out to be the worst day at work she'd ever experienced, and working for Aiden on a good day was quite a challenge.

Once, and only once, during the long day did he for even a second lose the cold and snapping tone he'd been using since they returned to work. He'd asked her to get the file on James so they could review some of the early numbers on the campaign they were working on, and she'd accidentally mumbled something about how she was sure that the Penthouse Prince's assistant didn't have to put up with being snapped at like that.

"You know how I hate it when you mumble," Aiden said.

And she met his eyes across the desk. For a second—a brief moment that might've been less than a second, if one were to measure it in real time—his mask slid away, and she saw her Aiden in there. The man with the smile that crinkled lines around his eyes and who said her name like it was his salvation.

But then the shutters snapped back into place, and he asked if she had the file up yet.

After almost ten hours in his presence, she wanted nothing more than to curl into her bathtub with a romance by Sara Arden. Maybe she could rinse her tears and troubles down the drain or at least forget about them for a little while. Get lost in a story and remember why love was worth the trouble…

But he called a staff meeting of all the top-level security clearance employees, so she ended up sitting at his right in a conference room instead of heading home.

He reviewed a few more plans with them, went over the coming week's schedule—busy, of course—and she coordinated all of the information, selecting what could be shared with which department and how those emails would be worded.

She was ready to shatter by nine that evening, and she closed her office door with a snap before crumbling to her knees on the carpet. How could she go on like this? How could she work by his side even one more week and pretend none of what they'd shared had ever happened? At least she had a little more time here to smooth things over and make sure Aiden would be okay.

Her earpiece beeped, so she scrubbed her face with both hands and took a few deep breaths before tapping it to answer. "Chelsea Houston," she finally said.

"Miss Houston," Aiden said, his voice too calm. "In appreciation for your service this weekend, I'd like to offer you the option of ending your employment today. I'll offer you paid leave as you fulfill the end of your two weeks' notice."

She swallowed. He was scared, but she'd show him he could still rely on her. "Thank you for the offer, Mr. Kelley." She barely restrained herself from referring to him as Aiden. "But I promised I would be here for two full weeks, and I always honor my obligations."

After a moment, he said, "Very well, Miss Houston."

The click in her ear rang with a painful emptiness that left her trembling.

She really thought they had something, even if it was only for a moment. But he wanted her to just go away. Maybe he was right. Maybe it would be for the best if she did quit now. But she'd be damned before she admitted it to him.

Chapter Fifteen

Chelsea

"Are you going to spill or just keep shoveling ice cream in your face like an animal?" Kimmie asked. "Because either one is fine with me, but I gotta admit…when you called me over, I figured you needed someone to talk to. Not just a witness as you tried to eat your feelings."

Chelsea stretched her legging-covered legs toward the end of the couch, shoving Kimmie in the process. "I'm not eating my feelings."

"Looks like you are. And lately, you've been off. Like, I've never seen you like this. Usually, you're all work, work, work, Aiden said, Aiden said, Aiden said. Then you went on that trip, seemed all happy for a minute, and by the time you came home—"

Her best friend twirled a braid around her fingertip before narrowing her brown eyes. "This has to do with Aiden. Something happened on that trip. Oh my god, did you bang the Irish Prince and not tell me? You *did*. And something went wrong. Girl, you did not seriously have all that happen and not tell your best friend, did you?"

Chelsea took another bite of ice cream—a huge one—and was rewarded with an ice cream headache almost instantly. "Ow!"

"You deserved that," Kimmie decided. "That's what you get for keeping secrets from me."

"I didn't keep secrets from you. I kept secrets from everyone. Aiden is in an important position, so the press—" Chelsea began.

"Is this because I joked about posting stuff to social media? Because we've been friends since college. I figured you knew that was a joke."

Chelsea could've kept her mouth shut if it wasn't for the fact that Kimmie looked genuinely hurt. "Of course I knew it was a joke. I'm an idiot. I don't know why I thought not saying anything would protect his privacy in some way, but there is more going on than the press would even guess at…and it isn't just him that would be at risk, so I panicked and didn't tell you. I'm sorry."

"Why are you apologizing to me?" Kimmie reached over and got a finger full of ice cream out of the pint. After she popped it into her mouth, she stared at Chelsea. "Thought we talked about your backbone? If you can't tell me because it might hurt someone else, you can't tell me."

Leaning forward, Chelsea spoke slowly. "I could tell you hypotheticals. No names. That would probably be okay."

"Hypothetically, is his ass as great as it looks in photo shoots? No, don't tell me. I can't ogle him anymore if you're bumping uglies, so it isn't even fair to help me paint a better mental picture." Kimmie grinned at her. "Hypothetically, that is."

"Okay, so what if I said that I met a guy, one that I thought I knew but who was very different than I expected, while I was on that trip?" Chelsea paused for another bite of ice cream. Kimmie didn't interrupt her, a rarity.

"A handsome guy?"

"The most handsome," Chelsea agreed. "And dominant. Like, crazy sexy dominant."

"Were there handcuffs?" Kimmie asked.

"No handcuffs. Just…orders."

"That's hot." Kimmie grinned. "You deserved some hot, for as many hours as you work. Go on."

Just thinking about it turned her stomach, so she set the ice cream down on the coffee table. "Then things went wrong. The hypothetical guy? He has a daughter."

"What?! Wait, not going to freak out and ask to who or how I've never read about this in a magazine. Just gonna stick with Mr. Hypothetical and say go on." Kimmie waved her hand. "So go on. It was just getting really good."

"No, things were just getting bad. He never met the kid before, and she is ten. So they wanted to get to know each other, hence…the trip."

Kimmie chewed on a fingernail, clearly trying to puzzle it all out. She gave up, looking frustrated, and said, "Someday, you're going to tell me this whole story, minus hypotheticals, but okay. I'm following you. Doesn't sound too bad yet."

"We lost the kid in the Grand Canyon," Chelsea admitted.

"How do you lose a kid?"

"We were making out. Next to a tree…er, leaned up against it? Whatever, that part doesn't matter." Chelsea rubbed a hand over her face in frustration.

"Sounds like it must've, if you managed to lose a kid in the meanwhile, but I'm guessing you found the kid. Otherwise, I would've read about it, I'm sure." Kimmie reached for her hand, as if she sensed the story was going to take a bad turn.

"Yeah, we found her. But then he blamed me for distracting him."

"That jackass." Kimmie's judgement was fast and harsh. "How the hell was it your fault? Did you pin him to the tree and force him to play tonsil hockey?"

Chelsea couldn't help but smile. "I should've been paying attention, too, and all I could think about was him. He wasn't wrong. I did distract him."

Kimmie rolled her eyes. "Yeah, and I'm guessing he was doing a damn fine job *distracting* you, too. But that's neither here nor there. What happened next?"

"Long story short, we came back home and went back to work. He didn't forgive me for what happened, and now work is kind of hard because of it." Chelsea shrugged and sniffed, trying not to tear up again but wanting to cry until she'd emptied out all the tears pressing behind her eyelids. "He told me to take a leave of absence until he replaces me." She practically whispered the last part.

Kimmie tugged her into a hug. "You're worth more than that, Chels. All the money in the world can't buy someone as awesome as you, and if he is too dumb to realize it, then he's the one losing out."

"I miss them," she confessed. "I wonder how the little girl is doing. There was a cat— "

"A cat?"

"A cat. Black, scarred-up, old tomcat. He was amazing. And I don't know what happened to him. Did he keep him? Or did the cat go home with the little girl? I just…I miss the little family, and there is no logical reason why I should, since they're not mine, but…"

Kimmie pulled back enough to look at her. "Honey, the heart doesn't care about whether or not you should care. It just loves."

"I didn't want to care. I didn't want to go on that trip with them. I don't want a family, and I'm not even sure I'll ever want kids. Really, I lost nothing that I had, so why does it feel like...grieving?" She blinked fast as more tears misted her vision.

"Like I said, the heart doesn't care about what it *should* feel. It just loves. No matter what happens with him or the kid, I'm here. We're family. I love you, Chelsea-girl." Kimmie hugged her again, tight.

Maybe if she hugged hard enough, all the broken pieces would fit back together.

Kimmie was right, and she tried to comfort herself with the possibilities. She might still see him after she quit. He could visit, since he always insisted they were friends and not just coworkers. They could make it work—others had.

Not could, they would. She'd find a way.

• • •

The one thing that kept her going was the upcoming weekend. Although she planned to work Saturday, she only needed to be in the office for the half day. All the work she needed to do on Sunday, she could do remotely.

If she could just make it through—a glance at her watch proved time was crawling by, but it'd been a solid two minutes since she'd last checked the time—two more hours and seventeen minutes, she could go home. Curl up in her bed. Order some takeout. Snuggle under the covers and binge watch something she streamed until maybe, just maybe, she managed to distance herself from her heartbreak.

Because she'd accepted that was what this was. Heartbreak. She knew and owned up to her crush on Aiden before the trip—not surprising since he was hot, eligible, and universally acknowledged for his charisma. The trip had made this not only worse, but it had exponentially developed those feelings past crush and into the danger zone.

Part of her even thought she might have been falling in

love with him.

Which was stupid, something else she could own up to, but it was how she felt. Acknowledging those feelings would allow her to deal with them and get past the weakness. Or, well, so an internet search said. Lucy popped her head into Chelsea's office without announcing herself, and Chelsea leveled a glare in her direction.

"Can I help you, Lucy?"

"Maybe? Look, I don't know if this is going to be a regular thing, but Ms. Welles is here again, and she wants to see Mr. Kelley. So do I just let her go on back when she shows up like this? Because he has a four o'clock with that company in the UK scheduled…" Lucy lifted her hands in a helpless gesture.

"One moment," Chelsea said. She tapped her ear and connected to Aiden's device. "Mr. Kelley, Ms. Welles is here to see you. Would you like me to reschedule your four p.m. or ask Ms. Welles to wait?"

"Send her back," Aiden said.

He'd been like that all week. Short, to-the-point answers. None of their usual work banter in place, nothing personal… and he was killing her with it.

"Yes, sir," she answered.

She tapped to disconnect and glanced up at Lucy. "Send Ms. Welles back. He'll be ready for her."

"Um, the kid is here, too? So do I send them both back?" Lucy looked vastly uncomfortable, but Chelsea doubted she could feel nearly as ill at ease as she herself did.

"Ask Ms. Welles if she'd like to take her back or leave her in my office to wait, please, Lucy."

"Thanks, Chelsea."

Lucy vanished, and moments later, the knob turned again. Waverley entered the office, head down, and flopped into the chair nearest the door.

"Hey, kiddo. How you holding up?" Chelsea tried to keep

her voice casual and upbeat, but it was the first time she'd seen Waverley since their ill-fated trip. She'd really missed the little girl.

"Fine, I guess." The child dropped the messenger bag she'd been carrying onto the floor and slouched even farther into the chair.

"You look bummed. Want to talk?" Chelsea asked, telling herself she was a glutton for punishment.

"Kinda? I don't know. Mom says it will be okay, but I'm just… I don't know how I feel about the whole thing. And I can't talk to my friends about it. Something about the press? I don't know. All of it is really confusing to me." The kid looked positively miserable, and Chelsea wanted to give her a hug.

"Well, whatever it is, you can talk to me about it. I won't tell anyone, swear."

How bad could it be, really?

Waverley admitted, "Mom had him on speaker, and before you even tell me, she's told me a hundred times that people who eavesdrop don't hear stuff they want to hear."

"You overheard something? That is what has you upset?"

Chelsea stood and went around her desk to kneel in front of the child. Stroking her soft hair, she gave the kid a comforting smile. "Whatever it was, they might have said it out of anger or fear or any number of other emotions. Kids aren't the only ones who sometimes say things they don't mean. Grownups do, too. I promise, whatever you heard, it isn't that bad. She's still your mom, he's your dad, and you'll work out how to be a family. It is just going to take some time."

Waverley leaned forward and hugged Chelsea tight. She returned the embrace, worried when the kid sniffled a little. She didn't want to make her cry. "Thanks, Chelsea. I was worried, though, because Mom seemed annoyed, and Dad said they needed to talk about it … But, well, I don't know. Mom didn't seem happy."

"What is it, Waverley?" Chelsea asked.

"He said maybe they should get married now, and that's why we're here. He asked my mom to marry him, and she refused to answer... I just don't know what that means for me, you know?"

• • •

Chelsea

She'd kept her smile on, asked Lucy to come sit with Waverley, and managed to get away from the child before she crumbled, but with her hands on the gleaming marble of the women's room, she realized she was breathing way too fast. She couldn't cry—*couldn't*—because if she started, she didn't know if she could make herself stop. And if she didn't manage to stop breathing so fast, she'd pass out and knock her head on the sink and die in a bathroom. But she just couldn't seem to get enough *air*...

What, had she thought that, just because she hadn't found panties in his office this week, he'd changed? A sob broke free, seeming to crack her heart in two as it got clogged in her throat. That things were different? That he'd actually felt something for her? She was a fool.

Any feelings she had for him were manufactured by her, not given by him. It was all in her head, a giant fantasy woven by a lonely and overworked mind. Aiden Kelley was exactly who he'd always been—an alphahole bastard who used women and made money and otherwise wasn't what she should want in the first place.

But she *did* want him. A second sob hit the barricade of her throat, and she realized the horrible gasping sound in the room was coming from her. Tears splashed her flattened palms, and she shook her head as if she could shake away the pain in her chest. She'd known him for years and knew he didn't care about anyone's feelings other than his own.

He didn't give a shit about her and wanted her to quit early so he could be rid of her, not because her presence pained him in any way. He wanted the uncomfortable reminder that he'd banged his assistant removed. She was nothing more than that to him—an inconvenience.

Men like him married the Margo Welles kind of women of this world, not the Chelsea Houstans.

She splashed cold water on her face, and then she dried off and walked out of the bathroom. She didn't hesitate at her own office door, instead heading right toward the bank of elevators. As she pressed the button to call the elevator, she tapped her earpiece and waited as it beeped in her ear twice before he picked up.

"About your offer to quit immediately? I've reconsidered. Good-bye, Aiden," she said before yanking the stupid thing from her ear. It made her feel special, really, like so many other little things he'd done over the years. She'd been the voice in his head, the person he allowed that constant contact. It made her feel like he needed her, like she mattered to him.

At the end of the day, it was just another lie she told herself to make it seem like he cared.

She dropped it to the floor, pleased when her steps into the elevator brought her foot firmly down on the discarded plastic and electronics with a satisfying crunch.

No more. She'd no more let herself believe the web of lies she'd built around a man who, as of right that second, proved that he didn't deserve her idiotic devotion. She was done—with him, with his life, with his company. It was time she found something that made her happy, far away from anything and everything that had to do with Aiden Kelley and his company.

She didn't expect to see him. But his hand caught the doors before they whooshed closed. He shoved inside the elevator, and the doors closed behind him. Before she could speak, he'd hit the elevator stop button and trapped them both inside the metal box.

"Why are you leaving? We can find a way to work out whatever is upsetting you."

"I can't work with you anymore," she said. She wasn't able to summon even a little heat to give force to the words. She felt hollowed out, as if there was nothing left for her to feel.

"I need you," he said. He paused, and the weak portion of her—her heart, she guessed—hoped he'd finish his thought with an emotional plea. That he cared. Anything. Instead, he added, "We have a great working relationship, and this company needs you. You know how important you are to us."

Part of her wanted to believe him, to read between the lines and invent a love he clearly wasn't capable of offering. But her brain was functional, so she decided to squash her traitorous heart and said, "That's too bad because, for once, I'm going to do what I need. And I finally realized that what I need is to be as far away from you as possible."

An alarm began to sound, so she reached past him to release the stop and allow the elevator to move. He blocked her move, stepping in front of the panel. "You'll be in breach of the contract."

She felt her lips curl into a smile, but it wasn't a happy expression. "I can always make more money. Please, just let me go."

There was nothing else to say, really. He was going to marry Margo. Was staying out her two weeks worth this giant pit of pain in her chest? She raised a fist to rub at the spot, as if she could relieve the ache in her soul with her own touch.

She couldn't look at him. He apparently noticed this, capturing her face in one hand and tilting it up toward him. She still refused to focus on his face, choosing to keep her sightless gaze focused on his ear. Everything in her felt like it had shut down, slammed out of operation by his actions as easily as he'd stopped the elevator.

"Chelsea..." His voice seemed to throb out her name, sounding more like a plea than anything else. The way he said her name, it sounded like he cared. Even in this dark moment, her heart tried to find excuses for him. Tried to believe that he was capable of emotions like love and caring.

He wasn't. Her logic knew it, even if her heart was too stupid to realize it yet.

His hand slid around her neck, capturing her hair before he dipped his face to cover her lips with his own. She didn't respond to his kiss, if she could call it that. She simply stood there until he backed up with a frustrated huff. "*Chelsea*," he repeated.

Finally meeting his eyes, she whispered, "Shouldn't you be getting back to your fiancée?"

His expression went as empty as the hole carved in her heart. She reached past him, then hit the button to release the elevator into motion. In the quiet seconds of the elevator dropping to the ground floor, he said nothing. She could hear him breathing, a harsh sound that echoed in the small space. When the doors slid open, she stepped out into the atrium without a glance back.

If she looked back, she might crumble. As she came to the automatic doors leading to the street, she paused for only a second to whisper, "Good-bye, Aiden."

But she knew he couldn't hear her.

Chapter Sixteen

Aiden

He leaned back in his chair, trying to stay calm when he felt anything but relaxed. He guessed he should be happy that Margo hadn't left when he'd fled the office to chase after Chelsea, but he had a hard time summoning anything that could be labeled joy.

Margo faced him, looking flawless, as seemed to be her norm. Her skirt was short, creamy white, and her shoes were a crimson much brighter than her hair. Everything about her appearance spoke of money, power, and elegance.

He yanked his tie loose, trying to find more air. *Focus on the problem at hand.*

He'd only managed to come up with one solution to ensure he could remain part of Waverley's life full time—marriage. It was logical. If they were married, he'd see his child every day. Waverley would have both her parents full time. And Margo? She'd have someone else to share the sometimes burden of parenthood. Everything would work out easier, clearly a win-

win situation for them all.

"You never said why you needed the money, not really, and this solves that problem as well," he pointed out.

If someone asked him a month ago if he'd be willing to negotiate hard to convince someone to marry him, he would've laughed his ass off. For one, he wasn't sure he was ready for that sort of commitment. Secondly, he'd always pictured it being something like what his parents had—a relationship based on friendship, mutual respect, and most importantly love. That sort of thing didn't usually require convincing the other partner to agree. For three, he was Aiden Kelley—if nothing else, his name should've paved his way down the aisle when he finally got around to proposing to someone.

Instead, Margo rolled her eyes and re-crossed her legs in the opposite direction—a tell that she wasn't comfortable with their discussion, either. "Ignoring for a second the fact that I want a bit more money to secure the future of our child, I will point out to you that we do not love each other. No amount of money is going to magically change that. Last I heard, love, or at least a good dose of like, was required before you got married to someone. In regard to the money, it doesn't really matter why I want it, does it? Pretending the money is leverage in this conversation is not only insulting to me, it is proof that you're grasping at straws."

"Love is something people in our position can't afford, Margo," he pointed out. "We share a child. The right thing to do is for us to get married and provide her the life she deserves."

"Bullshit." Her lips twisted in an expression he was familiar with from her movies. In her characters, it generally meant she was drawing a hard line. He had a feeling it meant the same thing in real life. "How is getting into a relationship that would make us both miserable an act based in the best interest of Waverley? I don't know about you, but I've always thought it was a crock when people tried to say they got or stayed married for the sake of the kids. You want to do the kid a favor? Show them what real love is. Model that so that they grow up to demand nothing less for themselves. That is good parenting, not showing her how two people can survive being miserable for years."

She leaned forward, tapping his desk in obvious irritation as she seemed to warm up to her topic. "Love is something everyone deserves, and I'm not willing to sell myself short. This proposal is coming about ten years too late, Aiden. Back when we were together—for that brief shining moment that I thought we actually might have something—maybe I would've bought it if you professed your love and devotion to me. *Probably* I wouldn't have, even then, but I'll give you a definite maybe. As I said, though…ten years too late for that discussion to even make a bit of sense."

He tried to be reasonable, thinking through reasons that it would benefit the actress, but instead found himself touching the earpiece. Chelsea's voice wasn't there—and based on the elevator interaction, it wouldn't be there…maybe ever again. He needed to focus on Margo, but his chest was tight, and he kept thinking about Chelsea.

The way she'd laughed with carefree abandon when he'd been disgusted by the cat. The way she'd sighed when he touched her. The look on her face when he'd woken her with a kiss…

He tried to focus on the topic at hand. Which was kind of important, as it might frame the rest of his life. "Marriage is an institution meant to solidify the family unit. The only reasonable thing for us to do, since the paternity test came back proving I am Waverley's father, is to get married." He wasn't sure why he was insisting on it either, but it seemed like the right thing to do. He also tried, for a second, to imagine waking up next to Margo every morning.

He came up blank, but he supposed they'd have separate bedrooms. That was how a lot of powerful couples did it, after all, ensuring a good night's rest for each and only coming together to couple in a carnal sense when they desired it.

Intimacy, from his experience, was something saved for either the poor or the gullible. He wasn't gullible, and a relationship with Margo would offer them both clear benefit.

He took the earpiece out and dropped it on the desk, hoping that removing it would make him stop fantasizing that Chelsea might change her mind and stay. He told her to leave and was proposing marriage to another woman. Surely, he wasn't demented enough to think she'd put up with that and stick around.

But he really wanted her to change her mind. To revoke her request to quit and say she'd stay with him because she wanted to be there, not just because he'd asked her to stay. He knew she said she was going to leave, had told him so since before his life exploded with the Waverley situation, but he just hadn't believed she'd do it. They were a team…

Margo didn't even pretend to smile as she interrupted his dismal thoughts. "If I wanted to legitimize our relationship, don't you think I would've told you about her sooner? Look, I'm going to be really upfront and forthright with you, Aiden."

"That's a change of pace," he mumbled snidely.

"Do you have to mumble?" the model asked. He jerked, shocked to hear those words from her. Had his Chelsea rubbed off on him that much? Was he talking to himself, now?

"I wanted Waverley. I didn't care about what *you* wanted or needed ten years ago, and maybe that was greedy of me, but I still can't picture you wanting her like I did," Margo admitted. "Was that wrong? Yes, and I'm sorry, but I can't undo the choices I made back then. What I can do is agree to share her with you now, if that is sincerely what you want. What I cannot do is pretend that I think getting married will be a good thing for me, you, or her. You don't want to be married to me, and Waverley wouldn't want us pretending otherwise."

"How would I know what Waverley wants? I only just got to meet her." He practically snarled the words, angry at himself for again attacking her but angrier with them both for not being able to wave a magic wand over the whole situation and make it pretty.

"Look, I think you already know her more than you're admitting to yourself. She said you guys were having a great trip and that you had some really good moments. She likes you, Aiden, something I never thought was possible. And, in part, from what she said, this is due to your assistant." Margo's smile was slow and almost feline, and he realized she knew she was scoring a hit with that sentence based on it alone.

"Leave Chelsea out of this. We're discussing us, not her."

Twining her fingertips together in her lap, Margo sat back and considered him for a moment. The experience made him feel uncomfortably like a bug under the microscope. "From what Waverley said, Chelsea and you seemed to be really close."

"Again, not discussing her. I'm discussing us."

"There is no *us*, Aiden. There is me and Waverley. There is you and Waverley." Margo's jaw set, as if she'd stated unchangeable facts.

"But there *could* be an us," he said slowly and softly. "That's what I've been trying to tell you. Waverley needs a father." What he didn't say but thought was, *she needs me.*

Margo stood, straightening her skirt. "You're right. For years, I denied it, and again, that was probably greedy of me. But she does need you, and I think you need her."

He stood as well, holding his hand out. "Finally, something we agree on. So when would you like to meet to set up the wedding arrangements?"

Margo's lips curled in a smirk, but she didn't shake his proffered hand. "I agreed that she needs a father, not that we needed to get married. She needs a father. So be her dad."

Without another word, Margo left. Frustrated, Aiden punched his desk and then turned to face the bank of windows behind him. He was alone again—as usual. It never really bothered him to be alone before, but then again…Chelsea was always there. Literally, she was the voice in his ear. When the company was in trouble, Chelsea was there. When he was upset about something, Chelsea was there. For years, she'd been his friend and companion, yet now…when he was more unstable emotionally than ever, she was gone.

So…

No problem. He'd just call her. He picked up the earpiece and tapped it once, which should activate her earpiece. "Chelsea?"

"Chels?"

Nothing but static.

He threw the damned thing down on his desk and grabbed his personal cell phone. Whatever, if she'd removed her earpiece—something she never did before they said good night, normally—he could just call her. He dialed her number from memory, too impatient to scroll through his favorites to find her. Her line rang three times before going to voicemail. Frustrated, he pitched the phone. It hit the mahogany cradle of the globe, denting the wood and cracking the screen of the phone. "Dammit," he hissed, flopping into his chair. The reality of the situation hit him hard. He didn't know why to expect she'd be there, other than…well, she was always there.

"Dammit, Chelsea, why *aren't* we together?"

She wasn't there to call him out for talking to himself.

…

CHELSEA

She gave up on the idea of working for him again about as soon as she considered it. She couldn't face him, day in day out, knowing what they'd shared and dreaming up possible happy ever afters into infinity. Besides, if he married Margo, was she really going to sit across the desk from him daily? Knowing he didn't love her but he'd married her anyway? Wondering if she had a model-shaped ass print on her desk? Wondering if he told Margo to kneel…

No, those thoughts led down a dark and twisty path she wasn't willing to travel. Better to put it all out of her mind. Better to go on with her life and try to forget she'd ever met Aiden Kelley, not to mention shared anything with him above and beyond a business relationship.

Which was what landed her on the brass-lined elevator that shot toward the penthouse of one of the tallest buildings in the city. The wavering reflection in amber showed her looking calm, professional, and otherwise ready to go to work. Previously, they implied they would hire her, and she could go on about her life as if that whole Aiden Kelley fiasco never happened.

The doors dinged, and she crossed the marble floor to the desk where a receptionist waited. "I have a two o'clock appointment?"

"You're applying for the executive assistant administrative position?" the woman asked in a nasal voice.

"Yes, I am," she replied.

"One door down, take a seat in the waiting room. Someone will be in to review your resumé with you shortly." The woman pointed down a short hallway, so Chelsea headed that general direction. She found the waiting room and took a seat next to a girl who looked hardly old enough to be out of high school.

"Are you applying for the assistant job?" the girl asked. She smelled strongly of cheap perfume, and her outfit of jeans and a sweater didn't bode well for her interview.

"Yes," Chelsea answered.

"Me too. I'm, like, totally not qualified," the girl admitted. "My name is Leigh. I gotta admit, I only took this interview in hopes to get to see *him*. Do you think we'll get to meet him? If we do, I'm totally gonna ask for his autograph."

Chelsea opened and closed her mouth before biting her lip. Finally, she managed, "Do you mean Mr. James?"

"Yeah, like, oh em gee, am I right?"

Chelsea sat back in her seat and unlocked her phone in an attempt to curb further conversation. The girl, however, didn't feel the need to give up with so flimsy a barrier. She continued to rattle off the wonders of Mr. James and about twenty more OMGs before a guy in his mid-thirties joined them. The guy also took a seat and glanced at the clock on the wall. "I was almost late," he stated unnecessarily. "I'm so nervous. Aren't you terrified?"

Leigh admitted she was indeed OMG terrified, while Chelsea shrugged. She had met Mr. James before, so she had a hard time being scared. If he didn't hire her, she'd try someplace else. Besides, it was a job. Working for an employer who she wouldn't sleep with.

One who likely would be a lot easier to deal with than Aiden had been. Not a lot to fear, there.

"Hello, hello, people. You're here to apply for the assistant job, and from what I understand, I have about fifteen minutes for each of you." Camden James swept into the room, not looking at any of them but instead focused on his tablet. "Looks like we have too young, possibly the new hire, and…"

His gaze lifted from the tablet and zeroed in on Chelsea. "Chelsea Houston. This is interesting. I'll see you first. Follow me."

"OMG, why did he pick her first? Should I ask for his autograph now?" Leigh bubbled as Chelsea got up and followed Mr. James into his office.

"I don't know," answered the guy. "But I bet you five dollars you're the one he just proclaimed too young, honey."

Seating herself across from Camden, Chelsea couldn't help but notice the stellar view he had of the city—including the Kelley Enterprises building down the road. Clearing her throat, she said, "Pleasure to see you again, Mr. James."

"Just to be clear, I can't hire you, so you can drop the formality now, Chelsea." Camden steepled his fingers, looking at her with his lips twisted in an expression of consideration. "Although, I would *love* to hear why you're here instead of in Kelley's office."

She stood and turned to leave. "Sorry for wasting your time," she began.

"Oh, sit down. I already messaged Jeanie that you're here, and she'll want to say hello. We haven't seen you since the Christmas party Kelley threw when he was trying to get us to agree to the campaign." Camden tapped his fingertips together until she sat with a huff of air.

"You could at least say *why* you can't hire me. I do recall you saying that if I ever decided to work someplace else, I should apply to you before I went anywhere else." She crossed her legs and glared at the billionaire. "Something about my ability to not kiss ass was refreshing, if I remember correctly?"

"Yeah, well, that was before my pal Aiden messaged me that I shouldn't hire you as you were still under contract with him and on paid leave of absence. Which, by the way, has me very curious as to what is going on between the two of you." Camden raised his brows, the same brilliant speculation which managed to make him a mogul clear in his gaze. "Now, be a good girl and spill."

"You're not harassing her, are you? Because I'll hire

her just to spite Aiden if I'm given even the slightest reason to believe he's in the wrong." Jeanie James, Camden's wife, swept into the room, looking as gorgeous as always. Her sleek blond hair fell in perfect curls around her lovely face, only accentuating her warm smile. The woman had a grace about her and an easy friendliness that Chelsea always found refreshing. Why the woman chose to marry a man like Camden James was simply beyond Chelsea's understanding. She seemed kind and open-hearted, while her husband was a well-known shark among sharks.

"You *should* hire me. I can't work for Aiden anymore, and if he thinks he can keep others from hiring me, I'll move. Be a pal, Jeanie, and help me get out of Kelley Enterprises," Chelsea urged, only half joking.

"Look, don't turn the wife against me. She's already annoyed that I didn't let Lowe dicker for more money when we closed the Kelley campaign." Camden didn't look worried in the least, contrary to his words, and he rose to wrap a possessive arm around his bride. The way he laid a gentle hand on her stomach made Chelsea wonder if they were expecting a new member of the family.

"He could've," Jeanie agreed. "But ever since we got married, he's a big softie."

The Penthouse Prince whispered something in his wife's ear that made her blush, and their whole demeanor made Chelsea tear up. *Is this what we could've been like? If things had been different…*

"Hey, you're looking bummed, and I'm sure it isn't my fault, but Jeanie will say it was. Tell Papa Cam all about it, and I'll go beat up Aiden for you. His face is too pretty for a man anyway," Camden said, coming quickly to her side.

"Nothing. It is stupid, and I'm a fool, and again, I'm sorry for wasting your time." Again, Chelsea stood to leave, but Jeanie caught her arm.

"You got involved with him, didn't you?" Jeanie asked.

The tears spilled over, although Chelsea was working so hard to keep them in. "No. Ridiculous. What kind of dumb assistant gets involved with her boss?" The last came out in a warble, and she sniffed hard to try to regain her self-control.

"She got involved with him," Camden said. "No wonder he doesn't want me to hire her."

"Oh, hush, Cam. Go deal with your other applicants. We're going to have a nice girl-to-girl talk." Jeanie waved one of the most powerful men in the United States out of the room as if he were no more than an annoying puppy.

The man in question sighed deeply. "But I wanna hear what happened," he whined.

"Scram," his wife reiterated.

Camden left the room in a huff, and Chelsea used the tissue Jeanie provided to wipe at her nose. "I *didn't* get involved with him. I can admit to nothing of the sort. There would be a huge scandal if I'd done something that foolish..." Another sob choked her, and she wanted so badly to confess it all and ask someone else what to do.

But that was the problem with being an adult. Life didn't come with a manual, and no one else had the answers you needed.

"Look, you don't have to admit anything to me," Jeanie said, perching on the end of the desk. "But let me tell you a little-known story about how I met Camden and how inappropriately I behaved, then you can decide if you want to tell me about your problems. Sound fair?"

Chelsea sniffled and shrugged. It couldn't make matters worse, could it?

"We faked it," Jeanie admitted. "Long story short, our entire relationship was built on a lie."

Blinking, Chelsea tried to think of an appropriate response.

"You're looking shocked, but that's just because the media played it off like it was the biggest romance ever. We can thank Lowe, Cam's lawyer, for that. He's brilliant when it comes to spin. They saw a billionaire who fell in love with an ordinary woman—"

"You're hardly ordinary," Chelsea pointed out. "I mean, you're gorgeous. You're now the chair of a few foundations… you've accomplished a lot to be considered ordinary."

Jeanie snickered. "Yeah, like I said, that's all great press. But the reality was that we were complete strangers until Camden proposed a deal to me. Fake being his fiancée, because his actual fiancée was off boinking someone in Cannes, and he would give me an insane amount of money."

Chelsea snorted, tried to cover it with a cough, and ended up choking herself. Once she regained her composure—while Jeanie laughed at her and pounded her back—she managed to say, "Yeah, that had to suck. Getting paid a ton to fake being in love with one of the handsomest men in America. How *did* you manage it?"

Jeanie's eyes continued to twinkle. "Yeah, well, as you likely know, from working so closely with Aiden, handsome, rich, and powerful men are frequently frustrating, infuriating, and otherwise a bear to live with."

Chelsea couldn't refute that one.

"Anyway, somewhere along the way, the lie wasn't a lie anymore. I'm not sure when, or why even, but that's what happened. Needless to say, it wasn't an easy road, but it was ours, and I wouldn't give up a single bump along the way."

Camden entered the room right then, looking a bit harried. "I hired the dude, gave the girl my autograph and a selfie, and I'm back. Are you talking about me?"

"Not every conversation is about you," his wife answered.

"But you *were* talking about me, weren't you?" His whiplash smile and fast talk always amused Chelsea, but his wife seemed to keep up with him just fine. On most of her previous experiences with Camden, Chelsea hadn't gotten to see how the two interacted as Jeanie wasn't there or left so that they could talk business.

On this occasion? Seeing the way neither could keep their eyes off the other? It was pretty easy to see that this couple hadn't fallen out of love...

But Jeanie's story painted another picture. If they were pretending the whole time, how would either know if the other was being honest? If it was all a show?

It made Chelsea's head hurt to try to dig through all the convoluted threads that particular web would create, which suddenly made her relationship—or what could've been a relationship, maybe—seem a lot less confusing.

"Yes, we were talking about you," Jeanie admitted. "I left out all the messy bits."

He bent to kiss her head. "The messy bits are where life happens."

"True," Jeanie agreed. "Anyway, my point in all this, Chelsea, was that whatever happened between you and Aiden—it is fixable. Most things are, really. The question you have to ask yourself is...whether or not it is worth the work. If it is, great. Go fix it. If it isn't, call me." Jeanie pulled a creamy white card out of her clutch. "Here's my card. I will hire you myself and make both the boys jealous."

"No fair," said her husband. "I should've called dibs."

Chapter Seventeen

Aiden

So far, the first visitation seemed to be going pretty well. Which was good, because otherwise the fact that Hematite had shredded the side of his couch would kind of not be worth it at all.

Not that he'd admit that he liked the wretched-looking cat. Even if he let him sleep on the bed. And even if his purr was part of what had been getting him through the long, sleepless nights of overthinking things.

"Do you want to go to a movie later?" he asked his daughter while passing her the drink she'd asked for. "I know, it has nothing to do with rocks, but there is a new movie that just came out, and it looks like it would be hilarious."

"I can't believe you're letting me keep the cat," the little girl said for the hundredth time. "I thought for sure that was a scam to win me over."

He scowled at her. "I don't have to win you over. You're my kid. You're just going to have to learn to love me."

"Whatever, Dad." Waverley rolled her eyes. "If you did want to win me over, Mom won't let me get my ears pierced. Letting me get that done would be major points in your favor."

"I don't think she'd be happy if I returned you with holes. So far, we haven't fought over anything. Do you want to be the cause of our first fight?" He was joking, but Waverley's face fell, looking terribly sad all of the sudden.

"Speaking of me starting fights, can we talk about Chelsea yet?"

"Nope," he said simply, turning away from her to put the orange juice back in the refrigerator. "What did you think of the movie idea?"

"You can't just pretend she never existed, you know. Probably that would be bad for my emotional growth or something. Like, I know a girl in my class who is in counseling…"

When the kid left the sentence hanging, he glanced over his shoulder at her. "Why does a kid your age even know that is a thing?"

Waverley shrugged. "Just throwing it out there, Dad."

"I'm starting to feel like you're just calling me that to butter me up," he admitted.

"Is it working?" Her smile was so like his own, he had to give her the points on that one.

"Okay, Chelsea and I had an argument. It wasn't your fault. Now she's looking for a job elsewhere. If I can stop her from finding work elsewhere, she'll probably be back from her leave soon." He hoped. Part of him was hoping the contract would be enough to bring her back, even though the fact that they'd had intimate relations could be used as a loophole to get out of it.

Not that he was sure what he'd do once she came back, but with each passing day, he was sure he'd made a mistake. He wanted her to come back to him.

Maybe *needed* wouldn't be too strong of a word to use. He really missed her.

"Wait, your idea of how to romance Chelsea is to just stop her from working for someone else? That's all you got? Wow, lame." Waverley shook her head, looking disappointed in him.

He sputtered for a second before taking a seat across the bar from his daughter. "For one, I'm not trying to romance Chelsea. She's my assistant."

"Your hot assistant," said the kid with a waggle of her eyebrows.

"She is—this conversation is so inappropriate. I'm calling your mother." He picked up his phone, but the child smacked a hand down on his to block him from lifting the device off the countertop.

"Look, Dad, if I'm not allowed to call her every time you annoy me, you can't do it, either."

He stared at her. "Fair point."

"Now, about you and Chelsea, sitting in a tree…K-I-S-S-I—"

"Stop that," he snapped. "We were not kissing. You never once saw—"

"I'm ten, Dad. Not a baby. Do you need help in how to date? Because I may be just a kid, but even I know hoping they come back to work isn't the most romantic thing a guy can do for a girl. Especially if you made her mad. Did you make her mad?" Waverley's expression said she thought he must have. "Just what I heard in the woods would've made me mad."

"Probably," he admitted. "I make a lot of people mad. It is kind of my thing."

She snorted, but she didn't disagree. He squinted at her until she giggled.

"I'm not taking dating advice from a ten-year-old," he advised her.

"Fine." She jumped off the barstool at the breakfast island and turned her little back on him. "Clearly, you know what you're doing and don't need any help from me, Waverley Kelley, romance doctor extraordinaire."

"Wait. You used my last name." He blinked at her, shocked.

"Uh, yeah. You're my dad. Anyway, no dating advice needed. Heard ya, loud and clear."

"Maybe I could use a little advice," he admitted.

Waverley grinned and grabbed a laptop. "First off, you need to watch no less than five romantic comedies and see how the heroes do it. If you want to be a hero, you have to learn *how* to be a hero."

He opened his mouth to disagree but then thought about it. Although he'd never before wanted to be a hero before, maybe that was what Chelsea deserved.

He thought about all the late nights she'd worked and the little things she did to make them bearable. He remembered her laugh. He remembered her asking him if he pitied her.

She was worth so much more than he was, really, yet she thought he might pity her.

"Good call, kiddo," he said.

They settled down for a movie day in—all romantic comedies—he even took some notes. Which was a good plan, as she wasn't satisfied with him watching the movies. Her finger hovered over the remote the entire time.

"Are you paying attention?" she asked at the first pause. "The name of this movie was *You've Got Skype*, and right now, the hero is at a point where he must do something. He knows something that the heroine doesn't, and it is make-or-break relationship stuff."

"Got that," Aiden said. "Picked up on it when he said, word for word, that she didn't know."

"Good," Waverley said, one hand on her hip as she stared

him down. "Now, if you were in his position, what would you do?"

"I'd turn the video on my end of the call and reveal myself as the hero," he said.

"Wrong!" she practically shouted.

"Well, that would resolve their issues. If they'd just been using video from the first call, this whole thing would've been resolved, don't you think?" He tapped his tablet, one eyebrow up, waiting for her to see the logic in his explanation.

"Dad, heroes don't do things like that. Again, grand gestures. Heroes have to prove themselves to the women they love." She looked exasperated with him.

"Seems sexist," he pointed out.

"Well, sometimes it is the other way around. Hang on, we'll watch *One Date with her Dermatologist* next. In that one, she has to fix things because she was living a lie." She minimized the screen to show him it was on the playlist.

"Can't I just take her to a ball game, put *I'm sorry, Chelsea* up on the screen, and wait for the kiss cam to focus on us?" he asked.

"Does Chelsea like sports?" his daughter asked. She seemed to be considering the idea seriously, so he perked up.

"No, but—"

"That won't work, then. In all the movies, the gesture fits the woman. If she was into sports, okay, but… What does Chelsea like?"

He considered the question for a moment. "Coffee with no sugar, because she's on a diet. Rocks. Leaving dinner parties the minute we can escape. Reading." He shrugged. "Me."

"Well, does she like you right now?" Waverley sat back down next to him, putting one hand on his knee.

"I don't know," he said. He hoped so.

"We're going to assume she does, then, until you learn

otherwise. What does she like to read?" Waverley asked.

"Romance novels."

With a giggle, Waverley clicked play on the movie. "We may have to watch more than five of these, then."

• • •

AIDEN

She wasn't answering his texts. Based on his lessons in becoming a hero, he needed her to talk to him before he could do anything further, but the woman was staunchly ignoring his attempts to contact her.

When he began the campaign to win back Chelsea, he thought the hard part was going to be getting Waverley to agree to his game plan. It seemed his daughter was very opinionated, and just about everything he thought of hit her nope radar. But he'd finally managed to come up with an idea he could actually pull off, and it got the kid's thumbs up.

Staring at his phone, he realized the entire plan was going to go to shit if he couldn't get her to agree to meet with him. He sent her a final text, this one likely more revealing than any he'd tried up to that point. "Chelsea, I just want to talk to you. Give me two minutes on the phone, please."

He cupped the phone in both hands and lay down on his bed, waiting to see if she'd finally respond.

When it rang, he dropped the phone on his face. Collecting himself, and cursing at the pain, he finally managed to answer the damn thing. "Hello?" he practically growled.

"You still sound like you're in a bad mood."

He hadn't realized how much he'd missed just the sound of her voice until he heard it again. Blinking fast, he said, "I'm not. I want to see you."

"I don't think that would be wise..." Her voice drifted off, and he wondered where she was. What she was doing. If she missed him, too.

"Do this for me, and I'll stop interfering with your job hunt. I'll formally release you from the contract. Hell, I'll call James Enterprises and give you a reference."

She snorted, and he wasn't sure if it was because she didn't believe him or if there was some other punch line in his phrasing. "Fine. When and where?"

Chapter Eighteen

Chelsea

It wasn't her first time visiting the museum, but it was the first time she'd visited when the stairs weren't littered with a crowd of people either entering, exiting, or loitering. A sign on the sidewalk proclaimed the museum closed for a special event, and she briefly thought she'd made a mistake.

Before she could double check the message from Aiden, she caught sight of a familiar little redhead. "Waverley?" she called out.

The vibrant young girl practically hurtled herself at Chelsea. "I'm so glad to see you. I've missed you!"

She smelled sweet, like childhood and energy, if she could bottle those scents. Hugging her little body close, Chelsea blinked back tears. "I've missed you, too," she admitted, surprised to realize how true the words were.

"I get to be your tour guide! Let's start in the fossils and stuff, okay?" Waverley didn't slow down, snagging Chelsea's arm and tugging her to follow whether Chelsea wanted to or not.

"The sign says the museum is closed," Chelsea pointed out.

"Not for us. Come on." The little girl moved fast, so Chelsea jogged to keep up. Barreling through the front doors, the child nodded to a security guard who doffed his hat at her. "Hi, Gary!" she bubbled.

The guard's face cracked into a smile. "Hello, Waverley. Remember, don't touch—"

"The displays. Got it." With a glance back at Chelsea, Waverley explained, "You were right. People do like it when you use their names."

She'd forgotten even telling the child that but recalled she'd done so in the museum in the Grand Canyon. That she remembered warmed Chelsea further. Exchanging an amused smile with the guard, Chelsea followed Waverley as she led her toward the prehistoric section of the museum. From mammoths to cavemen, the glass revealed the people of the past posed in various activities.

Blinking back unwanted tears for a second time, Chelsea got annoyed with herself, but she couldn't stop the emotions. It seemed doubtful to her that prehistoric women had met men as frustrating and blockheaded as men of their day and age. Then again, perhaps her problems were timeless, based on an artist's rendition of one cavewoman's frustrated expression.

But then one of the cavemen moved. Chelsea shrieked, automatically tucking Waverley behind her. It took her a second, but then she realized it was him.

Aiden.

"What on earth are you doing?" she asked him.

"Me caveman. You pretty."

She blinked at him. "Please tell me you don't expect me to take anything you have to say seriously right now."

He wore what was little more than a scrap of leather,

which—as pathetic as it made her feel—he did manage to pull off. His strong legs, his thick shoulders…

The flaw in the whole thing was that she never for a second doubted that they both agreed he was hot. Like, his attractiveness was never in question, not at any point in all the time she'd known him. What was in question was her sanity in thinking a man like him was actually interested in beginning a relationship with her. He stepped toward her, and she stepped back and away from him. "I thought you were going to entertain a genuine conversation about my contractual obligation to your company and me escaping those clauses which allow you to stop me from working elsewhere. If the best you have is a leather toga, we have nothing to talk about."

With those brave—and mostly heartfelt—words, she spun on her heel and led Waverley away. "I told him you wouldn't be into cavemen," Waverley admitted.

"You knew about this plan? Of course you knew. Do me a favor? Tell me what is next so I can avoid it."

"How do you know there is a 'next?'" Waverley asked innocently. She blinked up at Chelsea with hazel eyes just like her father's, right down to their expression.

"I was the one who said you could keep the cat," Chelsea reminded her.

The child sighed. "Probably we should take the elevator, then."

Chelsea didn't know what to think. Maybe he was scared she was going to sue him for harassment? There was no other logical explanation for his display or his texts. *You're the voice in my head*, he'd texted.

She cried at that one, though, to be honest, since he was basically saying what she'd felt for a long time. Via the earpiece, his voice had been with her just about all day, every day, for years. When they'd touched on the trip, he'd made her feel so damn special…

But that was stupid. He'd proposed to Margo. He was working on establishing a relationship with his child. She was nothing more than an employee—a *former* employee, if she had her way.

"So, when last we met, he'd proposed to your mother. May I ask when they're planning the wedding?" Chelsea asked. She wasn't able to look at Waverley when she asked, but she couldn't resist asking. Especially since it seemed he was trying to entertain the idea of an affair—was that what this was?—with her while planning a wedding to another woman, and he'd involved his child in the fiasco…

"Oh, he's an idiot," said Waverley.

"Don't call your father an idiot," Chelsea corrected automatically. Then she focused on Waverley's face. "Wait, what?"

"Probably he should've started the conversation with that, and I figured he'd texted you about it, but, well, Mom totally told him no way. They're not getting married." Waverley seemed unconcerned with those facts altogether, but Chelsea wasn't fully convinced the child wasn't at least a little bummed about it.

"I know you weren't sure what to think when we talked at the office, but every kid wants their parents to get together and live happily ever after. Are you even a little bummed she said no?" Of course, her saying no also meant that it wasn't Aiden who'd stopped that blessed union. Meaning he still would've gone through with it.

Meaning anything he said to her was basically hooey, even if part of her did go just a little soft when he'd said she was pretty.

She could recognize herself as a fool and still resist behaving like one, she reminded herself.

Waverley was playing some game on her phone, catching digital creatures, but she looked up at Chelsea with a sideways grin. "Yeah, I didn't want them married. Is that horrible? Maybe I'm a horrible kid. But, look, here's how I see it. I'm greedy. I've been an only kid my whole life. I've had Mom to myself for years, and I don't really want to share. Is that horrible? Meh, probably." The child shrugged.

"Yet you're here at the museum helping him with… whatever this is?" Chelsea said, leaning on the wall even after the elevator dinged. The doors opened and closed, but neither of them tried to get off.

"Yeah, well, like I said. I'm greedy. Dad came as a package deal—I talked to you before I talked to him. I like you. I want to keep you, and if he's willing to cooperate…you're like a bonus in a video game. If he does this right, I get to keep my mom plus I get a dad, plus I get a Chelsea. Blame it on me being an only child. I want it all." The kid smirked and didn't look remotely apologetic.

"Huh," Chelsea said. "Interesting."

"Plus, it means I get more presents for holidays. I Googled it," the kid admitted.

"Huh," Chelsea repeated.

"You're not convinced." Waverley put her phone in her back pocket and faced Chelsea. "Do you like my dad?"

Chelsea opened and closed her mouth. "I don't know," she finally admitted, trying to be honest but not wanting to upset the child if she had to leave.

Was she falling in love with him? Maybe a little in love with him for years before she'd actually gotten physical with the man? Probably. But did she *like* Aiden?

He was frustrating and stubborn. He tried to control everything and sometimes was the most selfish man she'd ever met.

But at the same time, he'd served in the military. He called his mom, even when she forgot to remind him. He found out he had a kid, and his first reaction was that he wanted to get to know her.

He also had women's panties in his office and treated women like they were disposable…

Except *her*. For years, he'd been a huge part of her life. He'd called Chelsea repeatedly when her aunt died, finally visiting her when she'd not come right back from her leave of absence. And on the trip, he'd kissed her…

Kneel. She could still hear in her head the way he'd said it. See the vulnerability on his face when he'd asked her why she'd called pause. Still hear the way he'd laughed at her finger moustache, all carefree and adorable.

"Yeah, I like him," she admitted, and even she could hear the hoarseness in her voice.

"Cool. I want to see the medieval gallery next, and so do you. Knights and stuff. Come on." Waverley punched the button, and Chelsea followed her, still thinking hard.

Yeah, maybe he'd told her to take a leave of absence, and maybe he'd blamed losing Waverley on her, but he was also all those other things. Some were good, some were bad, but the whole package was Aiden. If she wanted to care about one part, she had to accept him for all his jagged bits and awkward eccentricities. Maybe that was what being in an adult relationship was all about—not just being attracted to someone and caring about them, but caring about them despite their flaws.

But all of it was a practice in futility, because she still didn't know how he felt. Or she did, and it was that he wanted her to go away. Maybe she could believe he was attracted to her—although it was beyond her why he would, considering—but to believe he cared about her like she did him? That was a stretch.

One of the knights moved in clunking steps toward her. Nearby, Chelsea heard a giggle. She glanced over to see America's Sweetheart, Margo Welles, sitting at a banquet table in jeans and a designer blouse. Her hand was over her mouth, and she watched the knight—clearly Aiden—struggling to make his way down the hallway.

"Your dad is weird," Chelsea admitted in a whisper.

"I'm picking up on that," Waverley said. "Your tour ends here, by the way. I'll recommend that you head to modern history next. And if things don't work out..." The little girl looked at her seriously. "I talked to my mom. She says she'd like you to come to dinner sometime. Said that if I liked you that much, she would love to get to know you."

"I'll keep that in mind, kiddo."

The knight in clunking armor reached them and panted as he held out one hand. "Milady, this posy is for you."

Rolling her eyes, Chelsea accepted the flower and headed back to the bank of elevators. She needed a second to herself. A moment to think.

• • •

AIDEN

The armor had been a bitch to get into, and it wasn't any easier to get out of, but none of it was nearly as frustrating and confusing as his thoughts over the past week. When he'd had the conversation and movie day with Waverley, he probably romanticized the idea of Chelsea, something he recognized. When they came up with their plan to surprise her?

He'd still been thinking in Valentine's Day mode—some overly commercialized and idealized perception of what relationships and love should be like.

But when he'd been alone in his bed, stroking an ugly cat and thinking over his life, he had to face a much more brutal reality of what love meant. What was he giving up if she for some reason gave him a chance? What would he gain?

In the end, he made a list. Sure, he understood himself

enough to get that anxiety and his need to find control in a world filled with chaos drove a lot of his decisions. When he slept with women, it usually had a lot to do with physical craving and not a lot to do with anything deeper. Again, control, anxiety all mixed up in a soup of poor choices and the search for power.

But when he was with Chelsea, he became less and more than his sum parts. At work, she was often the one person willing to go toe to toe with him and say that he was making a bad call. She was the only one who understood him enough to try to make the mundane shocks into something he could handle stress free. She was also the first to castigate him when he banged strange women in his office and left the debris around like lace confetti.

Over the course of their little road trip, the usual barriers to them becoming more dropped. He was out of his element, out of his office, and they were able to face each other on somewhat equal terms. Technically, he'd still been her boss, but by even asking her to go, really, he'd conceded that she meant more to him than anyone else. After all, he was trusting her to help him build a relationship with someone he wanted to love for the rest of his life—his daughter.

That there was sexual attraction? Well, with Chelsea, that was really the gravy on top of an already tempting plate. She fit his life, even in the dark corners where jagged bits hid.

Pulling on the dress pants, he heard a tap at the door behind him and glanced down to make sure everything important was covered before he called, "Come in."

"Hey," Margo's voice said from somewhere behind him. "I'm going to head out with Waverley. She claims you two need privacy for this part of the conversation, and I don't even want to think about why she assumes that."

Her soft laugh made him turn to face her. "I'm sorry I didn't try harder back then. That I struck you as the kind of man who would walk away from his child, if he knew about it."

Margo's characteristic smile faded to become a more neutral expression he couldn't quite read. "I didn't know you well enough back then to begin to hazard a guess as to how you'd react. The best I can say is that I was young and didn't think about how my actions would affect you. Literally, I think I figured what I did didn't matter to you at all. I get," she began, holding a hand up to keep him silent, "that wasn't fair and, like I admitted before…greedy. But for what it is worth, I'm sorry. You seem like a good guy."

"Thank you. And thanks for bringing her today. It only seemed right, since she got to know Chelsea on the trip and all, and seemed so invested in me making right the damage done when I lost her—"

"Still can't believe you lost our kid in the Grand Canyon in the dark, but go on…"

"Yeah, well…I'm learning."

"Can I make a confession?" Margo asked, tucking a lock of her thick red hair behind her ear.

"Sure, why not?" He buttoned the shirt fast, not bothering with the sleeves. The quicker he got into the suit, the faster he could get to Chelsea.

"I dropped her once. When she was about one? I don't remember exactly, but we were snuggling on the couch, and I dozed off…and she rolled onto the floor. She wasn't hurt, but I was traumatized as hell. Oh, and once in a store, I was talking to a woman I knew from work, and Waverley was right next to me…and then she wasn't. Took me about two minutes, which felt like a hundred years, to find her inside a rack of shirts. Her giggle gave her away."

He stared at the model. "Why are you admitting all this?"

Margo shrugged. "Well, parenting isn't easy. We all make mistakes. My mother, she's been awesome ever since I had

Waverley. She once said it wasn't about whether or not we made mistakes; it was about how we chose to fix them."

"She sounds wise."

"You can meet her at Thanksgiving," Margo said with a snort. "Now, let's fix your tie, and you can go find your princess, Irish Prince."

"Don't call me that," he whined.

With a laugh, she gave his tie one final adjustment and left with a smile. While Aiden turned and headed up the stairs…

Hopefully to catch his future.

Chapter Nineteen

Chelsea

The modern stuff had never been her favorite part of museums, especially not art museums. She saw the value and craft behind the work, but for some reason, the softer stuff always appealed to her more. As a matter of fact, she had a large Van Gogh print hanging in her bedroom.

But she wandered down a hallway, surrounded by stone and art and her own echoing footsteps, and couldn't help but wonder at why Aiden had gone through so much trouble. It wasn't like he couldn't replace her at work—hell, there were probably dozens of people who would like her job and be qualified for it, and a few of them could probably do it better and without growling at Aiden.

Maybe.

And although the sex had been good—great, the best she'd ever had, mind boggling—the man was a playboy. He got sex from all kinds of people and probably had it hotter and better and…whatever.

She sniffled a little, becoming emotional because to her… all those things mattered. A lot. He always had mattered, even when she tried to convince herself he drove her crazy and it was just a crush. When she thought of living a life without him in it, she couldn't help but get sad. How was she to know which would be the last laugh she shared with him? The last kiss…

And then he was there, standing in his business suit and looking hot as hell. He stalked toward her in that lazy, sexy way he had. As if the whole world was his and, yes, Aiden Kelley had decided to grace them with his presence. He looked like everything that made their relationship impossible in that moment—suave, charismatic, rich, powerful.

He pulled a single red rose from behind his back and offered it to her with his familiar grin. "Hey, Chels," he said.

And her heart stuttered a bit, clenching in her chest as if unable to continue beating if she turned this man away.

So she did exactly that, even though it was hard. She turned her back on him and continued to put one foot in front of the other. Would it be tough—seemingly impossible—to go on in a world without Aiden Kelley? *A resounding yes.* Would it be sheer hell to see his face on TV and in magazines and know he wasn't for her? *Oh, yeah.*

But she could do it. Her father raised her to believe that she had value and, dammit, if he didn't realize that, he didn't deserve her.

"We left off on a bad note," he began.

"Ya think?" she asked sarcastically. "You don't get to be charming. You don't get to play nice." Her voice rose as she warmed up to her topic. "I've been a dedicated employee for years. I've been here for you for years. I even went on that crazy trip with you. And you? You…" Her voice cracked a little. "You *hurt* me."

"Okay, a worse than bad note. For one, I wanted to let

you know that I overreacted to the Waverley situation and shouldn't have blamed you at all. That was all on me, and I even knew it at the time, but for some reason I blamed you. Easier, I think, than shouldering the whole burden at the time…but worse in the long run. Can you forgive me?"

She didn't turn to face him, instead pausing to consider a statue. "I blamed myself, so I felt I deserved that one. No apology needed."

"Which is all the more reason I shouldn't have blamed you," he said. His hands came down on her shoulders. She didn't flinch away, but she didn't face him, either.

"Yeah, well, I didn't fault you for doing so."

Silence filled the museum, only the tick of a distant clock and the sound of their breathing to break up the otherwise weighted soundlessness. His hands didn't move, and neither did she. She felt like she was waiting for something, and, although she wasn't sure what it was exactly, she knew she needed to give him time.

Again, she noticed that they even seemed to breathe at the same time, synced on some deep level she couldn't ignore, even if she was forced to walk away from it.

"There's more," he practically whispered. "I have had feelings for you for a long time. I can't even say exactly when they started, but they were always there. I don't know if you could tell, but I trusted you in a way that I've never trusted anyone outside my family. I guess what I'm saying is I tried to show I cared by letting you in, but I also tried to stay safe."

"Safe?" she asked and then damned herself for interrupting. What if he didn't continue?

"Safe," he repeated. "I told myself you were an employee, so every time I had thoughts about you which might seem inappropriate, it was easy to tamp down on them. To tell myself I was avoiding a harassment suit or how unfair it would be to you to have the creepy boss hit on you. I told myself this, I think, to protect me, not you. You see, if I admitted how much you meant to me, it put me at risk. I wouldn't risk losing you, and I didn't risk messing it up. I had this nice safe spot where I got to have you in my life, the voice in my ear, but I didn't have to give up anything to keep you there."

"Well, you paid me, so..." She snickered, but he squeezed her arms slightly with his hands, and she went still.

"Then on this trip, I held you in my arms. I got to see, for a moment, what a full life with you might be like. And it was even better than I might have imagined. Which was scary as hell, because if it didn't work, it meant you could walk away at some point." His voice broke a little, and she pinched her eyes closed on the tears that had overflowed.

"I've never walked away, Aiden. Even when you were frustrating and drove me so crazy that you made me talk to myself. And when I needed to leave, for my own sanity, you wouldn't let me." She lifted her arm, dislodging one of his hands, to wipe at her nose.

"I know that. And I don't want you to walk away at all. Please stay with me, Chels. I'd really like to date you," he admitted.

She sniffled again, bracing herself. This was the moment. She got to decide if she'd give this a shot. He'd given her the choice. With a deep breath in, she slowly turned to face him.

...

AIDEN

He felt like he was holding his breath, almost dizzy waiting for her response. He'd never laid his own wants out like that, not admitting so many vulnerabilities, to any person. It left him feeling vulnerable. Edgy.

She could shatter him with a word.

He released her as she moved to turn around and allowed

her to face him, and for a second, he was tempted to squeeze his eyes shut. To hide from her, since his words left him feeling naked.

But he didn't, so when she turned, it took him a second to compute what he was seeing. "Is now really the moment for a finger moustache?"

Her lips twitched. "Felt right."

"I'm going to take that to mean, 'Oh, yes, Aiden. I can't resist you any longer. Take me now, you glorious beast of masculinity,'" he said.

She snickered. "Yep. Totally what I was thinking."

But he couldn't joke anymore, so he simply moved her fingertip. Digging his hand into the soft sweep of her hair, he tilted her head and took her lips. Nothing felt so much like home as Chelsea's mouth. She tasted sweet—like cinnamon and apples—and when she let out a little whimper, he hardened so much that his cock ached.

"I need you with me," he admitted. He peppered kisses down her neck to her collar, nibbling the sweet flesh there as her nails scraped his scalp.

"We're in a museum," she reminded him.

"I like to have sex in odd places," he reminded her.

"They have cameras," she added.

He glanced around and groaned. "Probably a good point."

"Do you have a car?" she asked.

Her soft brown eyes met his, and he was pleased to see how hers were glazed with desire. "Hell yes, I have a car."

Like a couple of horny teenagers, they continued to kiss on the elevator. He almost managed to get his hand up her skirt before she swatted his hand. "Cameras," she reminded him again.

"Why did I think this was a good place for your grand gesture?" he asked her. Scooping her off her feet, he strode through the museum lobby, giving the security guard a nod as he held open the door for them.

"My grand gesture?" the tempting minx asked as she toyed with his buttons and smiled.

Once he had her in the back of the car, he knelt at the floor near her feet. "Yeah, Waverley had me watch a bunch of movies to figure out how heroes won their ladies. Seemed kind of silly, but they all did something really romantic to woo the woman in question. The best I could come up with was the museum thing. I wanted you to see that I didn't just need you for work but that I want something more with you. I don't just want sex with you or you to work for me, although I do want those things."

"You also want finger moustaches," she said.

"I want to laugh with you. I want to reach for you when things get tough, and I want to be the thing you reach for." When he saw she'd started to tear up, he leaned forward to take her hands. "Yeah, I'm not doing any of this right. You're not supposed to cry, dammit."

She moved to the edge of the seat, catching his face and capturing him with a kiss. Usually, he liked to be in control—to be the one to give orders when things got sexy. In this case, however, he found more reward in his own surrender than he would've in controlling her.

"One sec," he panted. His breath was coming fast, and his body ached to have hers under him. "To my house," he said into the intercom connecting him with the driver.

"I thought you liked to have sex in weird places," she said. "Not into doing it in the car?"

"No," he said, surprised to find the truth in the word. "I want you in my bed. I want time with you, time to explore you. I want you so weak with need that you can't think of what your name is, not to mention noticing things like where we are."

He nibbled at her fingertips between words, pleased when

he heard her tiny gasp as he sucked one digit into his mouth.

"We're here, sir," came over the intercom.

It had seemed just moments since he'd gotten her into the car, but he'd noticed that about his time with Chelsea. Time seemed to buzz by, and he hadn't a clue where it had gone. He'd been lost in her—her flavor, her scent, the way her lips turned red and ripe from his kisses.

She didn't let him carry her inside, instead laughing as she ran ahead of him. That was okay—she could run, so long as it was his bed she headed for.

Once inside, he didn't more than close the door before he spun her and pinned her against the intricately carved wood. He stripped her of the shirt, pulled her breasts out to rest in the cups of her bra, and all of it with his hand shaking like some kid on Christmas morning who just found out he'd gotten the very best gift of all.

The feel of her soft body against him had him grabbing her ass, pulling her closer as he again kissed her. He could kiss her forever.

"I have to admit…I kind of hoped we'd end up like this," she admitted.

"Me too," he said.

"I dressed for it, even," she whispered. Her cheeks flushed with color, darkening the freckles he wanted to taste one by one.

"Oh yeah?" He cupped her breasts in his hands, pulling one closer so he could suck the nipple deep into his mouth before nipping it gently. "How so?"

Her groan was his answer, so he swept his hands under her skirt, urging the fabric upward. When his hand slid between her legs and encountered hot flesh, already moist with her desire, he let his head fall to her shoulder with a small moan. "You're not wearing panties. You haven't been, this whole time?"

"Yeah. I don't know, thought it might turn you on."

"Fuck," he whispered, sliding his fingertip against her tight little bundle of nerves. She arched into the touch, bucking against his hands. "All I'm going to think about every time I see you from now on is going to be me wondering whether or not you're wearing panties. You realize that, right?"

Her smile was full of feminine mystery, but then her hand cupped his already hard cock. "Good."

With one arm, he lifted her until her legs wrapped around his waist. She bent, kissing him as he kept her in that position until he'd managed to maneuver her to the living room. He'd never make it up the stairs without taking her. "I need you now," he whispered.

She'd managed to get his jacket off, and his shirt hung from his wrists. "Good," she echoed, biting down on his nipple as he lay her down. "It is my turn to be greedy."

"You deserve better," he began, but she'd managed to undo his pants.

"I deserve now," she said. When she stroked him once, held tight in her small palm, he couldn't think of a reason to disagree.

He never managed to get his shirt off. Or her skirt, leaving it banded around her waist like a chunky belt when he filled her. She clawed at his back as he thrust inside, careful to keep up his gentle teasing of her clit until she screamed out his name.

"Aiden!" Her cry sounded like forgiveness and forever, all in one sound.

"Chels," he whispered. And because he was weak with needing her, because he couldn't imagine ever wanting another as much as he wanted her in that second, he reached for her.

Her arms were around him; their mouths merged; when he exploded with pleasure, he felt it from the hair on his head to the balls of his feet.

Unable to do more, he bent his head to rest it on her shoulder, breathing hard with exertion and shaky with pleasure. Little muscle movements deep inside her continued to rain sparkling shocks of pleasure through him, but he tried to remember how to move, worried his weight was crushing her.

Her hand smoothed his hair, and her lips rained kisses across his neck and ear. "I won't leave you again," she promised.

Finding his strength, he stood and carried her upstairs. They had a lot of lost time to make up for, and he wasn't wasting a second of it. "I won't give you reason to."

Chapter Twenty

Chelsea

Her hands were sweating. She couldn't do this. She spun and turned to flee but was stopped by a four-foot-tall, red-haired ball of energy. "If I can't back out, you can't, either," Waverley said.

"You literally can't. You're related to them," Chelsea pointed out. "I still can escape. It isn't too late for me."

"Yes, it is, actually." Aiden wrapped his arms around her from behind. "You're both chickens."

Waverley's eyes narrowed to slits. "I'm not a chicken."

"Then go meet your grandparents," he replied without missing a beat.

The little girl squared her shoulders and whispered under her breath, "They're going to love me. I'm absolutely adorable."

Chelsea overheard her pep talk to herself and broke free from Aiden's embrace to kneel before the child. "You *are* adorable. How could they resist you? Plus, they've got ten years of spoiling to make up for. This is going to be awesome."

Without warning, Waverley wrapped her arms around Chelsea and whispered in her ear. "Thank you. And I have my piece of quartz you gave me in my pocket for luck."

Enjoying the child's hug, Chelsea breathed her in deep. "You got this, kid."

Waverley released her and stared up at her dad. Her voice was monotonous, as if she was proclaiming her doom, when she said, "Well, they're *your* parents. Lead the way."

"She's bossy like her dad," Chelsea pointed out. Aiden shrugged and smiled before turning to walk up the neat sidewalk toward the cute little two-story house. When Chelsea pictured where one of the richest men in the United States' parents might live, it wasn't something like this house. Then again, not a lot about Aiden fit into what she might have imagined, so why would his parents be any different?

She lingered back, giving Aiden and his daughter plenty of room to enter before her. If she had her way, she'd hide on the wide wraparound porch and rejoin the group when they left. Aiden promised them ice cream, if they were good, and a special "grown up" treat for her later…

If she survived that long.

The door was opened by a short woman who looked a lot like one of those sweet grandmothers off a commercial. All neat as a pin and smiling. Behind her, Chelsea could see what looked like an older version of Aiden—same hazel eyes, same build, but with gray hair. When the woman moved, Chelsea could see that Aiden's father was wearing a long-sleeved turtleneck gray sweater and one of Aiden's first products, The Useful Kilt.

She lifted her hand to stifle a giggle. Aiden's dad was quite handsome, for an older guy, and she couldn't help but wonder if Aiden would age just as gracefully. The grandmother was hugging Waverley, who was talking a mile a minute.

Chelsea backed down another step off the porch, but it was too late. Aiden spotted her. "Mom, I brought Chelsea along, too, although she's trying to sneak away. She's a chicken," he said, pulling her to his side by interlocking their fingers.

"Traitor," she whispered before turning a bright smile toward the older couple. "Pleasure to meet you."

"Finally, you bring her home? Sweetheart, the bracelet you sent for my birthday was just lovely. Thanks so much!" The woman moved forward and enveloped Chelsea into a hug.

Chelsea tried to think of an explanation—something that would make the woman think that the gift was from her son, for instance—but came up with nothing.

Instead, she glared at her boss and, when his parents turned to lead Waverley inside, kicked him in the shin.

• • •

AIDEN

He stood in the doorway to the kitchen, watching as his dad pulled out the old train set. Something about the old toy had a charm which captured Aiden as a child, and Waverley proved no more immune to it than he had. As he set it up, the child examined each car and discussed what they meant with her grandfather.

Aiden could tell they were going to get along great. Behind him, he heard the gentle clunk of dishes and water. His mother preferred to do them by hand, still, and Chelsea had volunteered to help out after dinner. The women's voices were soft, a balm, and Aiden couldn't help but think that, although he hadn't planned things to work out the way they did, he couldn't have asked for more than that one moment of perfection.

He wanted to offer to help, but he could tell his mom was

peppering Chelsea with questions—getting to know her—and didn't want to ruin the chance for them to get to know each other. Plus, it was a good excuse not to do dishes.

He wasn't a fool, after all.

When they'd finished, he caught Chelsea from behind for a quick hug and dropped a kiss on her neck before she escaped to the bathroom. Knowing her, she had to text Kimmie an update, so she'd be in there for a minute. Staying behind in the kitchen, he glanced over at his mother who was watching her husband and grandchild with a smile of her own.

"So do you like them?" he asked his mother.

She turned to face him, hands on hips. "What kind of question is that? I'm assuming, as you brought that girl to meet us and haven't with any of the others, that this one is one you might be keeping?"

He nodded. "If I have my way, yes."

"About damn time," she growled. Chelsea came around the corner just in time to hear his mother swear, and her eyes went wide. "You've been talking about Chelsea for how long now? *About damn time*, and that's the best I have for you, Aiden Ellis Kelley."

She caught the shocked look on Chelsea's face and waved her hand in dismissal. "Oh, dear, don't look shocked. You work with this lot; you can't pretend you're offended by a little rough language."

Chelsea's laughter made his lips twitch. In seconds, he was laughing so hard, he was bent at the waist. His father peeked into the kitchen and asked, "What'd I miss?"

"Just me welcoming this girl to the family," his mother said. Pulling Chelsea into another hug, she said, "Welcome home, Chelsea. I always wanted a daughter, and he brings me a daughter and granddaughter in one night."

Aiden smiled, but then she narrowed her gaze on him. "And you? Meet me on the porch."

She headed that direction, but he paused by Chelsea on his way through. She was tearing up. "Don't cry."

"Did you hear what she said?"

"Yes, and that's why I said don't cry." He dropped a kiss on her forehead. "Be right back."

She sniffled again and swatted his ass. "Go get 'em, tiger."

"Don't ever do that again," he warned her.

She smiled unrepentantly and went to help with the train.

On the porch, the night was crisp and the crickets were chirping. He glanced around at the neatly situated neighborhood—a far nicer place than the one he'd grown up in. When he'd offered to buy his parents a house, he thought they'd choose to live in the city, near him.

Instead, they'd asked for this. A quiet place, filled with small-town charm, even though it was in the suburbs. "What's up, Mom?"

He leaned on the railing to the porch while his mother sat on the swing, moving her legs gently. "You're going to marry her?"

"Hopefully, one day. For now, this is enough. When I think she might say yes, I'll probably ask." He didn't lie, not to his mom. She would've seen right through him if he'd tried.

"Good. I have a bit of advice, if you'll hear me out."

He hadn't expected any less. His father was the one who teared up, who loaned him money, who tried to fix things in their family. His mother? She was the dragon at the gate.

"You need to remember to put that little girl first." Her green eyes narrowed on him. "But based on the way the two of them interact, I'm going to guess Chelsea wouldn't have it any other way."

He smiled. "I got lucky," he admitted.

"You did." She folded her hands neatly in her lap. "That wasn't all I wanted to say."

"Okay."

"Don't waste a second of it."

His mother teared up, and he rushed across the porch to sit next to her on the swing. "Hey, no crying. This was a good night."

"I know that," she snapped. She rubbed a hand across her nose. "It goes by faster than you think. Just a moment ago, you were a little boy, playing with that same train. Then you were off in the military, and I lost nights of sleep...wondering where you were and if you were safe. When we came to this country, I didn't think I'd have to give up my boy to keep the country safe, and we got lucky there, too. You're still here. You've built a wonderful company, and I can't say how proud we are, but none of that will keep you warm when your hair turns gray and your days run short. So don't waste a moment of this time you have with either of those girls. Love them hard, because that's what matters. The moments."

He hugged his mother and promised, "We'll come visit next weekend. Whenever I have Waverley, I'll visit, and we'll come home more often."

Her smile was slow and devious. "And I didn't even have to ask. I told them my boy was a clever one."

Epilogue

AIDEN

The packed ballroom nearly overflowed with the elite and wealthy, everyone putting their finest jewels and designer clothing on display as if to prove their worth. But Aiden Kelley wasn't swayed by any of it. He shook the hand of those who made it a point to warm his palm—from bankers to CEOs to actors—because work required him to keep up his end of the facade, but there was only one face in the crowd he actively sought out…

The one he couldn't quite see. He knew she was there, though, both because she'd promised to meet him and because he could almost sense her presence. Love was funny, and if it was crazy to need her so much, sign him up for his own padded room. He'd happily be crazy if it meant another day with Chelsea.

A hand clapped down on his shoulder, and he glanced into the eyes of Camden James, the notorious Penthouse Prince. "What's up, man?" Camden asked. "Heard you were planning to tie the knot. Congrats."

Shaking the other man's hand, Aiden couldn't help but grin. "Yeah, the press hasn't shut up about it. Apparently, or so I've been told, it is okay to date your assistant but not to fall in love with her." He shrugged.

That kind of thing might have once mattered to Aiden—the illusion, after all, must be maintained. But somehow the idea of impressing strangers didn't hold a candle to the idea of impressing Chelsea. After all, without her, none of it would mean anything.

Camden barked in laughter. "Yeah, I'm still rather bummed about that. If you'd just kept pissing her off for another week or two, I might have gotten to hire her. Why'd you have to make things right again?"

"Because I found the one thing I didn't want to learn to live without." He might not have shared that tidbit with others, but from what Chelsea had told him...Camden and Jeanie had been there for her when he'd messed everything up. He'd owe the other man for that, even if the debt remained unspoken.

"I always thought you were an all right guy, Kelley. Nice to be proven right once in a while. Say, did you hear they are still calling you by that nickname, too?"

Aiden frowned. "The press?"

"Yup," Camden said before taking a sip from his champagne flute. He scanned the room, but when Aiden followed the direction of his head...he saw Camden's gaze had settled on his new wife. Now rounded with child, Jeanie James looked as gorgeous as ever—the perfect picture of a wealthy wife. Rumor had it, though, that Jeanie was the head of a foundation that focused on helping kids. Supposedly, she wasn't the typical trophy wife and instead spent her time trying to make a difference.

Aiden made a mental note to mention the foundation to

Chelsea. They'd probably get along great, working together on a project like that. Plus, it would likely do Chelsea good to have someone to talk to where she didn't have to worry about the press. From what he'd seen, Camden James made sure his wife was well protected from the media.

"Yeah, the press." Camden rolled his eyes, making his derision for the whole thing rather obvious. "They're still calling you the Irish Prince."

"That's your fault, isn't it? Once they made you a prince, it was only a matter of time before they started giving the rest of us silly nicknames." With a grin, he drawled in the voice of his family's homeland, "But a bit of the magic of the old country isn't a bad thing, is it, lad?" He winked at Camden, who outright laughed at him.

A hand slipped around his arm. "Have I mentioned lately what it does to me when you speak with that accent?"

He turned away from Camden, backing his love up until they were in a somewhat private corner. Grinning down at her, he softened his voice before whispering, "I'll take you to the emerald hills of my homeland, show you the sun setting over the ruins of a castle, and then sit with you in my arms by a bog fire to warm your tender flesh."

Chelsea visibly shivered, her eyes going a bit glazed in what he recognized as her desire. "Dude, not in a ballroom. You have terrible timing." Although she scolded him, she went on tiptoes to kiss his chin.

"It isn't terrible timing. It is all the time. I never stop wanting you." He took her lips, delving his fingertips into her hair where he could feel the promise of her warmth. Their tongues tangled, and he was pleased when he left her just a little breathless.

With just a kiss, after all this time.

"Pause," she whispered. It was their code now, for when they stopped being what the world needed them to be and when they wanted to become what they only were when they were together. "What do you say we ditch this party? I'll teach you a new game..."

He couldn't disagree with her proposition, as games with his assistant happened to be his very favorite way to pass the time.

Dragging his fingers through her hair, he cupped the back of her head and kissed her again, not caring who saw. He saw the flashes past his closed eyelids but didn't care what the world thought of his actions. After all, the press could say whatever they wanted about them...

The woman who was the voice in his ear, in his heart, and who spoke to his body was in his arms. He'd found the woman he'd turn to if things went swirly. Somehow, that made the rest not matter so much. For her, he'd be the knight...the caveman...

Even an Irish Prince.

Acknowledgments

No writing happens in a void, so these are just a few of the people who helped me while I was writing this one.

As always, thanks to my kids, Justice, David, Ashton… I couldn't do it without you. Between food when I'm on deadline to just making me smile, you make all this possible. Love you so much. You're my heart.

Thanks to Michelle and fam for things like emergency groceries and surprise lunches. Love you bunches. Thanks to Tony for his Sunday grocery runs and constant belief in the stories.

Thank you to my mentor, Barb, for reading above and beyond what you had to and for being so great.

Thanks, as usual, to Sara and Heather. The fact that you read and cheer me on…I can't begin to say how much that means to me.

Thanks to Joe-La, Vanessa, and Tamar—couldn't have written this and dealt with my first semester of grad school without you.

Thanks, Tony & Dar and Jamie for my new floors. You made my home lovely and breatheable. <3

Thanks, Ryan, for conversations and beer.

About the Author

USA Today Bestselling Author Virginia Nelson is the hybrid author best known for *The Penthouse Prince*. Aside from that, she's the mother of three wonderful biological children and tons of adopted kids and critters. Virginia is a graduate of Kent State University with an Associate of Science and a Bachelor of Arts in English and a current student at Seton Hill University where she's pursuing a Master of Writing Popular Fiction. Sometimes called the rainbow unicorn of romance, she's also far from perfect and she knows it. You can find out more about her—including where to find her on social media—on her website.

Books for sale. Snark for free.
virg-nelson.com

Discover the* Billionaire Dynasties *series…

THE PENTHOUSE PRINCE

Discover more category romance titles from Entangled Indulgence...

Romancing the Bachelor

a *Hamilton Family* novel by Diane Alberts

Eric Hamilton isn't looking for love. But then Shelby walks into his life, and suddenly, he can't think about anything else. Unfortunately for him, she hates his guts. But he's a man who loves a challenge. Shelby Jefferson can't wait to get out of the city, and back to her country roots. The last thing she wants is to fall for another man who might make her want to *stay*. But Eric is nothing if not persistent, and before long she's falling for him. Hard. But history repeats itself, and she has to choose between a man and herself—again.

The Millionaire's Temptation

a novel by Sonya Weiss

Holly Campbell is trying to turn her life around. But, to protect her younger brother, she has one last job to complete. All she needs to do is use her unique skills to break into the safe on a yacht—millionaire Jake Lawson's yacht—a man Holly had a one-night stand with before she knew his true identity. Jake knows Holly can't be trusted. He believes she used the one night stand as a decoy to steal from his company and he knows she's up to something again. Jake's determined to figure out what and stop her. He won't let her take anything from him, least of all his heart.

Playing the Spanish Billionaire

an *International Temptation* novel by MK Meredith

Playing as a local tour guide for the hotel reviewer Mateu meets seems harmless. But when London discovers her charming guide is really CEO of the hotel, she plays along to see how far he'll go to make her dream vacation unforgettable.

CPSIA information can be obtained
at www.ICGtesting.com
Printed in the USA
LVOW03s2117211217
560430LV00001B/17/P